EXTANT

BRIAN GATTO

SEVEREDPRESS

EXTANT

ISBN: 978-1-922861-12-2

CHAPTER ONE

It was crushing him.

Trevor Morris was contemplating strangling his co-pilot, Bradley Rickshaw. The first hour alone was hard enough to endure. If the thousands of pounds of pressure outside did not make him implode, then the nuisance of a human being such as Rickshaw would make him explode. All the man did was smack his gum and burp. Belching Bradley is what they called him. He lived off soda and other high carbonated beverages.

The worst part was the fact that there was no such drink aboard. It was an after-effect of his consumption prior to disengaging from the ship that made him gassy. Now Trevor was stuck with him.

It would be another three hours before they even reached the Mariana Trench. Their descent would only be for a couple of hours though. Their mission was not to reach the bottom. It was to scour and search near the entrance.

Suddenly, Bradley burped again. It was the loudest one so far. He did not look away like a sheepish schoolboy or coy prankster. He embraced that he was a disgusting pig. All Trevor had done thus far was wrinkle his face and cover his nose. That expulsion of gas was the last straw.

"Will you knock it off?!"

"Oh, bite me, princess," Bradley chuckled.

"Man, how did I ever get placed in this cage with you?"

"Cages have gaps, unless you want to implode?" Bradley sneered.

"You know what I mean!"

"Well, that's what you get for switching shifts."

Trevor had to admit that Bradley had him there. Jacob Dalton asked to stay aboard the ship because he fell off and Trevor offered to take his place. Now he was stuck, miles below the surface, with a renowned gas producer. He just hoped Bradley would not turn to expelling methane before the trip's end.

What is more, it was his day off. He was not only a fool to sacrifice his relaxation time, which was already exceedingly rare, but taking the gig in the first place. He began to wonder how Bradley even got aboard. They must have chalked it up to him always being gassy. If that were the case, Trevor was going to have a word with the guy's up top.

Pop.

Bradley cracked his gum.

"You're starting to get on my nerves."

"Just starting to?" Bradley laughed heartily.

"Don't laugh or you just might erupt," Trevor mumbled.

"I can't help if this pressure makes me burp."

"Yeah, sure. Let's just blame the pressure," Trevor scoffed.

His co-pilot heard him but paid no mind.

An hour and a half of grueling gas later and they were nearing their destination. When the vast nothingness first appeared, both men were quiet, motionless. After a while, they had gotten used to it and began to shift in their seats more. Some smaller bioluminescent creatures began to appear. Soon, a plethora of undersea life came into view.

"Lots more than usual down here, huh?" Bradley said nervously.

"Why're you worried? It'll make our job easier."

"Yeah, well. Doctor Platt needs to be more patient. We aren't equipped to keep diving the way we've been."

"You think I don't know that?" Trevor shot back.

"I just think that, with this much life around us, there must be a reason. We usually don't see some of these species until we're down at least another ten thousand feet." Bradley pointed out his observation window. "Like that goblin shark should not be up here. They are usually found a little over four thousand feet down."

Trevor looked at the depth gage. It said they were nine thousand feet down. He then adjusted for the feet they were at from the peak. They were technically only two thousand feet into the trench.

"Wrong kind of shark we're looking for anyway," Bradley finished.

Silence fell between them again. Oceanic particles and life flew and fluttered past the minisub. Bradley wanted to say something more. If Jacob were down here, he mused, he would not be so testy. There was so much to enjoy down in the trench, but Trevor never fully embraced that. He would rather be working on the minisub and not driving it.

"Look, I don't want to sound like an impatient bastard," Trevor began, "I just hate having to come down here. Even though I designed and built the damn thing, this submersible is still in the tinkering stages. She's a testy bitch . . . simply put."

"I get it." Bradley paused. "But without Platt we'd have no job and without this sub we wouldn't be able to carry out that job."

Trevor took a deep breath and then exhaled. "I guess you're right."

"Watch out!" Bradley shouted.

Instinctively, Trevor braked and turned right, narrowly missing a slithering object. "Whoa!"

Neither man had time to process what they saw. It was too fast. They both checked the systems, and everything seemed all right despite the rough tilting action her captain had just performed.

Righting the submersible back to its original position, Trevor turned on the fish finder. The signal beamed back in the form of a glowing green signature. Its proportions came through and at a measurement of fifteen feet. Both men ogled at the reading. It was snake-like or something akin to an eel.

"What the heck is that?" Bradley asked.

"Only one way to know for sure." Trevor steered the ship northward towards the direction of the signature.

He then flicked on the beams to their highest setting. A light shot outward and created an illuminated haze in the water. Something had obviously been near for there were bubbles as if they had been filtered through gills.

In the surrounding sea, a massive number of its inhabitants fluttered towards the lights. Some nibbled, others examined, all were interested. Their forms danced around excitedly as if they were putting on a show. Then, just as soon as they were there, they were gone.

The two kept a keen eye out but it was impossible to decipher black from black beyond the beam. Like a bull charging a red cloth, the creature rushed for the minisub; its bristled teeth showing further and further down its gullet as its jaws opened wide.

"Hard left!" Bradley screamed.

Trevor wasted no time, turning the vessel as it narrowly evaded the serpentine creature.

"What the hell is that thing?!" Bradley cried out. "It looks like a fish from a nightmare!"

"I think we found our specimen." Trevor grinned from ear to ear.

"What?!"

"You heard me! Quick! Get to the hatch! We need to capture this animal and then get the hell out of here!"

"But it's not my turn," Bradley whined.

Trevor turned to his co-pilot. "It's for the job and Mr. Platt." He winked as if to say *gotchya*.

Bradley unbuckled himself.

"Look out! Here it comes!" Trevor shrieked.

The man nearly fell on his rear. He quickly found his way back to his chair. When Bradley looked out the observation window, there was nothing there. "Your asshat!"

Trevor burst out laughing.

"Oh! Now look who is in high spirits!" Bradley spat.

"Just get to your post!" Trevor said behind a chuckle.

Opening a compartment, Bradley unstrapped the Velcro from a display and then unclipped it from across to prevent the weapon from falling. The tranquilizer had three shots. He loaded one into the chamber and then slung the gun over his shoulder.

Following this, he knelt on one knee and unfastened the hatch door. Thankfully, Trevor's design worked. Any other submersible would compress into the size of a soda can with the amount of pressure at this depth.

"You almost ready back there?!" Trevor called over his shoulder.

"Just shut the beams off. I've got it from here," Bradley reported.

Flicking the tiny switch, the water went dark. The only lights were the green, yellow, and red ones that signified what buttons were what in the minisub.

Bradley flicked on the flashlight in front of him and then placed the weapon in the water. He moved it back and forth in a meticulous motion and then turned it off. He then repeated the act a few more times before he began to see that something was coming up.

The ripples in the water were becoming increasingly erratic and it was not from his carefully placed movements with the weapon. Bradley placed the butt of the gun against his shoulder. A hideous mouth opened before him. The head was not small enough to get through the hatch, but it was enough to hold it in place for a few seconds. Long enough to shoot the tranquilizer into the fish's jaws. They instantly clamped shut.

Sliding back into the water, it began to sink.

"Okay, Cap! Get your claws ready," Bradley said as he stood and shut the hatch.

Maneuvering the minisub just below the animal, Trevor used the metal extender hands to get ahold of it. The grip was strong enough to bring it under the sun where leather strapping came out and then wrapped around it. They then squeezed but not hard enough to make the fish uncomfortable.

"Nice and snug." Trevor smiled.

"Good!"

"Yeah, now let's get the hell out of here!" Trevor laughed.

They both knew he was not laughing about the flawless capture so much as the fact that he would soon be away from Belching Bradley who was rearing up for another gas-attack.

Sinking behind the horizon as if it were disgusted by the day's so-called accomplishments, the sun was setting to close out another day. There was no shame to see its glowing form, but it threw out an eerie dread in its rays. At least, that is what Trevor figured. He always liked to apply human elements to inanimate objects. It made it easier to justify his anger when certain things got in his way.

The minisub had docked and the specimen was being stored in a tank. The containment was filled with saltwater forty by sixty-two feet and had a depth of five feet. It was enough to have their special guest slither around in but not let it gain enough speed to crack it.

Trevor noticed it did not matter too much now. Before, it had inertia that would rival a mako. Now it seemed subdued. It was looking around as if calculating where it was and trying to determine how to escape. Trevor could not help but find the thing creepy looking in a deeply unsettling way.

What was worse was that it never made eye contact with him. An underlying feeling of revenge visibly surged through its body. It was obvious that it was not happy being captured and now trapped. Still, it would not face its captors. Brooding was the least of its problems right now. It was as if it knew that.

A hard hand came smacking down onto Trevor's shoulder. "A job well done!" Bradley chuckled.

Shaking the hand off, Trevor turned to his co-pilot. "I think you're mixing a good job with bad taste."

"What is wrong with ya, man? We got the shark."

"Yeah, but why?"

"Come again?"

Trevor took a step closer to Bradley, much to his own dismay. He did not want to be anywhere near Belching Bradley, but he had to get his point across. "He could've picked a great white, a bull, hell even a dogfish for all I care. Why did he need an extinct species?"

"Maybe they have some hidden chromosome that the others don't?" Bradley shrugged, unfazed by Trevor's tense posture.

"Why would he need that exact chromosome though? What's even the purpose of this experiment?"

"Genetic testing, I don't know?" Bradley chuckled.

"That's just what I'm afraid of." Trevor turned and began towards the stairs that led up to the living quarters.

"You're forgetting one thing!" Bradley shouted after him.

Trevor turned to face him. "Oh?"

"The fish isn't extinct. It's extant." Bradley smiled and then waved. "Have a good night, Mr. Morris."

The two parted ways.

All the while in the laboratory, Dr. Morgan Platt watched from the porthole. "People," he scoffed. "They think too much."

He returned to the surgeon table and continued to study the dolphin in front of him. Lost in his own little world, Morgan began to cut into the neocortex in its brain. The level of intelligence of the dolphin was always something of an anomaly to him. He was often wondering what other creatures could prosper from such intelligence. The brain capacity would improve as would their problem solving and motor functions.

While poking at the tissue with a scalpel, he reached for his radio. He stopped himself, realizing his hand was covered in brain juice. *Damnit, hold on, let me change my gloves.*

He quickly did so and then sighed. *I sound like Trevor. It's always someone or something else's fault. It stinks too because I don't like Trevor.*

Turning on a golden oldie from Buddy Holly, he returned to his work. His admiration for this project was there but he knew it was only the beginning. Still, he had to press on. *Bradley has good dedication,* Morgan thought. *If I can just get him to take himself seriously, we could go far on this project.*

A whirring sound caught his attention. Blades whipped around in the evening sky as the chopper circled the battleship. Morgan growled. "Never enough time, always plenty of distractions though."

He stood up and walked outside.

A woman came off the chopper, her blonde hair whipped around her face. She struggled to keep it out of it while simultaneously taking her sunglasses off. Her long stride brought her straight to Morgan Platt. "How's the specimen?"

"Rather calm, it's alarming."

"I see," she said and then the two walked towards the holding tank.

In clear view, the shark was motionless but displayed obvious signs of its awareness. It still filtered water through its enlarged gills and swayed its tail back and forth.

"She really is calm, tranquil even," the woman observed.

"Yes, and I hope the modifications don't change that."

"What modifications are you proposing?" she asked.

"Which of the ones listed can I preform?" Morgan continued. "I mean, everyone from Peta to the FBI will be knocking on my doors, some more calmly than others. What is covered by the humane act and animal rights?"

"Again, what modifications are you proposing? I can take a wild guess that none of them would fly with anyone, but my job is not to assume."

"I predict amphibious attributes couldn't hurt. Still, I want to be sure they can even be brought to fruition. I have never dealt with a procedure like this before. This is something new that is being done on something alien as far as the human race is concerned."

"All sea life, even the ocean itself, is alien to the outside world. It's basically water space but on Earth." The woman gave a slight chuckle. "Now, I need to know what you plan to do with this thing.

Legal or illegal, right, or wrong. I think I can help you out."

CHAPTER TWO

The mighty sea.

As the thirty-foot deep sea fishing charter boat, the *Oceanic Titan*, plowed through the water, kicking up white spray and leaving behind froth trails, her captain, Professor Grant Dorset, smiled. It was a perfect sunny day with the temperature high at ninety-one degrees and the humidity was lower than normal. He attributed the weather to luck as he did every Monday to Friday. Over the weekend he usually slept in and did not care much for the outside world.

He figured he was in luck today given the beautiful forecast and he was going to need it. If the reports of the damaged sensors were anything to go by, it would be at least a three-hour job to fix them. He had hope though that it would not take more than thirty minutes including the dive and inspection.

There was a loud, continuous ping that sounded suddenly, and he looked over at a small device situated on the dashboard of the console. He picked it up and read out the readings on the tiny screen.

He wondered if the school would invest more money in this kind of equipment someday and not on passion projects that became headaches for him. As he finished going over the device, he realized that they were getting close.

Pulling the throttle downward, the boat began to slow but still drifted a bit with the tide it created. Wavelets lapped against the hull as Grant walked down the ladder. He entered the cabin where his two students, Adam Brisk and Jane Warrington, were preparing for the dive. They looked up at him and he nodded, the gesture signaling that they had arrived.

Grant watched his two students rather than the equipment. One of them was a resolute career woman who had everything going in her favor regardless of all the trial and error she had endured in the past. Her struggles would soon be over, and she would be on her way to getting grants for other expeditions in her desired field. The other was a guy who just wanted extra credit.

He was just thankful they both knew how to dive.

Adam had grown up in the Bahamas and spent a lot of time searching sunken ships. He always claimed that snorkeling was for tourists, and he was probably right. He was a native of the area and knew that his accent was hard to understand sometimes. However, he came from a rich family, and they wanted to put him through college. He rarely attended class though and, when he did, he was uninterested. Finding out he was failing near the end of this semester shook him good however and he begged Grant for any extra credit possible. He refused until Adam's father contacted a friend of his who was, in turn, friends with the dean.

Still, when Adam did go for extra credit, he was motivated. Grant figured the bored-looking kid before him now was just tiring of the long trip they had taken to get out here.

Jane had been a Cali-girl. Born and raised in the hills, she spent all her time down by the beach, soaking up the rays. One day, as she tells it, a handsome man came up onto the beach in scuba gear and she was instantly attracted. He relayed his profession and soon, she was more interested in diving than she was in him. He was kind of an uptight creep anyway. The idea of swimming in the ocean but being able to observe below caused her to sign up for diving lessons.

After a while of snorkeling, she started diving. She grew a passion for the underwater world and its inhabitants.

A few years later, she started college and the first course she attended was marine biology. She was able to get ahead and excel at a lot of the classes except she needed to pass basic English to get her associates. She struggled, she hated writing and was soon caught in a tricky situation.

Her teacher, Ms. Ritter, was not helpful, much less supportive. Grant found her in the halls one day, crying. She relayed her struggles and Grant offered to tutor her in exchange to attend his class next semester. Jane's whole face lit up. She had asked why he was doing it and why he wanted her in his class. His answer was simple. She had that look in her eye, one that Grant called the sea-spark. She loved that and agreed to his terms.

That was a year ago and they were still good friends and planned to remain as such even after the semester was over and she moved on to another college. She really wanted to do field work.

When Grant asked for a couple of students with experience in diving to accompany him on fixing one of the school's sensors on a Friday for some extra credit, Adam and Jane were the first hands to shoot up. Adam was in it for the grade while Jane just wanted to assist the professor any way she could.

Now they were near Cape Town, Africa, out in the Atlantic Ocean trying to fix the school's equipment. It was an easy job for a boost in grades.

Grant was not happy with it though. While he believed you had to show hard work and determination to be allowed extra credit, Young Springs International College did not see it that way. They only saw the money. Furthermore, he thought the college was weird all around. It was filled with art school majors and hipsters who wanted to make a comfortable living. It was even called Young Springs because the students got to take vacation in the spring. He often chuckled at the obvious name and thought it was common knowledge. It was called spring break for a reason. They were trying to be clever, and he got that. He just thought everyone was far too laid back.

He promised himself that after the semester he would relocate. He usually kept good on his word and rarely did things get in the way of it.

Finally, the boat came to a stop. He helped the air tanks onto his students' backs and then patted them on the shoulders. "Be careful down there."

"Sure thing," Jane said.

"I mean it. This area is known for great whites."

"Understood." Jane smiled reassuringly.

"I thought a great whites didn' like tha taste of human flesh," Adam inquired. "Or any of de sharks for dat matta."

"Great whites are notoriously aggressive here. Australia is facing the same problems as well. A lot of attacks."

"I thought Australia was a desert." Adam looked genuinely confused.

"You've been talking to the wrong people or watching the wrong shows," Grant continued. "Australia has beautiful oceans and plenty of fish in them. It is not known as one of the deadliest places in the world for just land-based animals."

"A'ight, I hear ya, Professor." He then turned to Jane. "Lez get dis show on tha road."

The two made their way out into the deck and then sat on the starboard side. Grant checked their gages. Jane had eighteen minutes of air while Adam had sixteen. He cursed inwardly. The college was really cutting corners. They did not even have their air tanks filled before taking off. It was a golden rule that, unless completely empty, the tanks would not be filled until after two trips. It went without saying which trip they were on.

Both Adam and Jane backdropped into the sea and then turned around slowly. They swam downward, the light haze in the water making it only mildly hard to see. Soon, they were near the bottom.

Shortly after, Adam spotted the cable and went to investigate while Jane checked the specimen traps, they had set up. They were a little invention by Grant and acted like underwater mousetraps.

They were metal tubes that had small amounts of bugs in a thin pouch on one end. Crustaceans and small fish would enter, and the back would seal shut with a green light illuminated on it to signify the capture.

Above, Grant began to lower a vacuum hose into the water. It touched downright next to Jane who grabbed it and put some of the trapped sea life into it. It led up to a tank aboard the boat.

Jane found another one with the green glowing light. It was getting to be well worth the trip. Usually, they were lucky to find two set-off traps.

She put the fish in the vacuum, and it was sucked up. Then something caught her eye. It was one of the tubes, but it had a red glowing light which meant something was stuck.

The tube was no longer than her hand. Most of the time, if something was stuck it would be an octopus or a puffer fish that blew outward too quickly and their spikes get hooked on or even impaled through the tube.

As she got closer, she realized it wasn't either one of those things. Instead, it looked like an eel of sorts. She wasn't quite sure what to make of it. She put the tube in the vacuum, and it was sucked up.

Aboard the *Oceanic Titan*, Grant picked up each tube and released the specimens either into the tank or over the side and back into the sea if they were not worth keeping. When the red tube came shooting up, he looked at it for a moment. It looked like a mangled mutation of sorts. It had a thick neck with gills that looked infected. It was also shaped like an eel. It was only a foot long but had to curl itself up to make sure it could fit. The red blinker was on because one of the bugs was caught near the exit. Its tiny head was crushed but still stuck to the door mechanism.

Grant couldn't quite figure out what the animal was. It looked like a cobra with its thick neck, but it wasn't a hood. A growth would be a more appropriate description.

He suddenly felt uncomfortable for his students and decided to ring the underwater bell attached to the port side as well as pull up the vacuum. Both would signal them to come up. It was going on for ten minutes anyway.

Below, Jane saw the vacuum go up and she turned to look for Adam. He wasn't near the cable as far as she could see. It did go for a distance though. There was a coral foundation nearby and she figured he must have gone behind. She expected the cord that connected the sensors together must have gotten caught up in the current because it was lying on a rocky bulge that jetted out of the foundation. She was certain Adam would be there and made her way over. It was a simple fix, so she began to wonder why he hadn't pulled the cord off the rock and placed it back down on the ocean floor already.

As she rounded the bend, there were little pieces of white particles or something floating around. They looked like snow or coconut flakes. When she got closer, they became thicker. Soon it looked like a cloud of sinew was everywhere. Then the thicker chunks came: flesh. They were small at first, able to hang out in the open. When Jane looked down, she saw huge chunks with faded red near the ends of each piece. It was obvious something had been attacked. . . Or someone.

Jane was quick to decide to try and find her classmate. She swam further as a red haze began to cover her. Blood was everywhere and she was having trouble seeing. It clicked in her head that this was a recent feast, but she was determined to find Adam.

She suddenly bumped into an object, and she let out a little shriek. The thing that lay before her was at least twenty feet long. Its black and white skin made it clear what it was, an orca. It had been practically hollowed out. She was able to make out several lines going around its girth. The hide was marked with rashes of some sort. Like something gave it the ultimate bear hug. It had been crushed so hard that its stomach had blown out.

Slinking back in grotesque horror, she bumped into another object. This one was much smaller. She spun around and saw Adam there. He pulled her away as fast as he could and the two made their way back towards the boat.

They didn't see the animal poke its head out of the orca's belly.

Both Adam and Jane surfaced simultaneously. Grant jumped when he saw them reach over the starboard side. He hadn't heard them come up. He crossed the deck and helped them aboard.

"What took you two so long?" Grant inquired.

"What is tha hur-ray, Professa?" Adam asked as he pulled his head piece off.

"I was just worried is all. That last specimen you guys sent up was definitely an odd duck."

"That's not all we found," Jane said.

"Ya, that one wouldn't even fit in tha vacuum!" Adam chuckled.

"That's not funny," Jane scolded him.

"What else did you two see down there?" Grant asked impatiently.

"T'was jus a dead whale. 'n orca," Adam said.

"Yeah, but it had weird injuries around its skin. It was like something had wrapped around it and constricted it to death," Jane explained.

Grant thought back to the specimen in the tank. "Let's get to the next spot. Then we can head back."

"Shouldn't we get back and report the carcass to someone?" Jane wondered.

"Who?" Grant continued. "It's not really our problem, Jane. If it were washed ashore, then I could see it. We're miles away from land. It'll be devoured by every little nibbler in the sea before it reaches it. For now, we'll head out to the next destination and then focus on the task at hand."

"Agreed, Professa, tha whale ain't good to no-a-one when dead and torn apart like t'at," Adam further drove the point home so that they hadn't a need to worry about it.

"It still doesn't feel right," Jane said shyly. She didn't want to be the voice of reason here.

"Look, if it will make you feel better, I'll call the coastguard and let them know. It is odd that it is stuck on the bottom so maybe they'll check it out."

"Okay." Jane gave a relaxed smile.

"Alright, let's get going," Grant said and then walked up to the console.

He pushed the throttle up slightly and then brought the boat towards their next destination where the second sensor was.

CHAPTER THREE

It was an odd sight.

On their way to look at the second piece of equipment, the sifter, a device that weaved through sand particles and rocks and kept living specimens inside so that it could sense through their motions, Grant noticed something. There was a small water-locked fishing village nearby as always but there was something else there too. A woman jumping up and down waving her hands over her head. It was a very peculiar sight.

That spot, which was built on a coral foundation and could be described, officially, as an atoll, had been uninhabited for years. Now, there was an African woman signaling from one of the docks. She was dressed professionally with a floral skirt, white blouse, and light blue, sleeveless jean jacket. Her braided hair danced around her waist as she gestured for them to come over.

"What's this?" Jane wondered.

"I'm not sure." Grant began to turn the boat towards the village.

"Whoa, man!" Adam said aloud. "Ya wants ta tell me whatchya think ya doin'?"

"I'm going to see if she needs help."

"I am figurin' tat. Imma more concerned about dem rocks. We be havin' to swim home if jus' one of dem hit the hull, man."

Grant turned to Jane. "Please get the dinghy out Have Adam help you set it up."

"I don' wan' any part of dis," Adam said. "Tis not wise to mess with other pepule's business."

"She wants us to be a part of whatever's wrong. Otherwise, she would not be flagging us over." Jane stood by the professor on this one.

"Whateva man."

Jane went inside the cabin and then returned with a bundled-up boat. Adam reluctantly went over and helped her when he saw her struggling. He had a grim look on his face that never went away. They finished setting it up and heaved it over the side.

Grant let the anchor down. There was no way he would let any of his students out of his sight in a shady situation such as this. The three boarded the dinghy and pushed away from the charter boat.

As they made their way, Adam held his disapproving expression. He did not talk, just stared ahead towards the village. There was no denying the situation was bizarre, but he felt there was more than met the eye.

Jane looked at him. "Lighten up, Adam. Don't be rude."

"Tis not me ya shoul' be worryin' about, yes?" Adam stated with an air of understanding.

He thought he was all knowing in this situation, but it was obvious he knew nothing about the woman on the dock's predicament.

Jane decided to pass the short amount of time it would take to get to the village by looking at the water below the speedboat. It was clear but not enough to be able to see the bottom. It was odd because the water had been much clearer further out. It signified that something must have kicked it up. She began to wonder if it was like another orca. She then looked up towards the village.

The woman looked to have tears of joy streaming down her face. There was no denying she had been through a hellish experience. One that, given her attire, she wasn't prepared for. She put her hands to her face and closed them in prayer. Things were getting weird and fast, first the specimen, then the orca, and now this. Whatever it was, Grant wanted to be done with it. They were not too far from the sifter and other sensor and figured they'd have this all wrapped up before the afternoon and be home by lunchtime.

That did not seem to be the way things were going to pan out.

Still, he was going to find the underlying cause of this. He wondered if she had any information on the ravaged orca but then figured that that was preposterous. Still, he tucked that little idea in the back of his mind. There was more than met his eyes. Things could always play out in a certain way in which he'd have no control. He who conquers knows his enemy.

The dinghy bumped against the dock lightly. The woman was quick to help secure the line that Grant tossed her. She then stepped back a few feet to allow them room to climb off. Once the three of them were on the dock she rushed towards Grant and hugged him. He was taken aback, dumbfounded even. She then began to sob uncontrollably.

"So, uh, what's going on here, Ms. . . ." Grant inquired.

"Cane. My name is Sasha Cane," the woman responded. "We need assistance."

"What seems to be the problem?" Grant pressed.

Sasha let go of Grant. "I'm not alone. I came with my employer to check on the status of our equipment. Blane and Caplin told us that everything was smashed but Patty wanted a further investigation and..."

"Whoa, slow down," Grant said. "Let's start from the beginning. You came with your employer to check up on something that was said to be destroyed?"

"Yes. We came a few hours ago. Things just got out of control and our boat sank when it hit the rocks and it drifted away after we made it onto the docks."

"I see. Who is in charge here?" Grant asked.

"Sasha," a female voice came from behind one of the huts. "Where are you?"

A woman with wavy, golden blonde hair came out from the corner. She too was dressed conservatively with a black suit and dress pants and a white blouse. Grant figured that she was Patty given her nature and the fact that Sasha had not mentioned any other female names.

"Ah, there you are," she said and then regarded the three new guests. "Who are these fine people?"

Sasha composed herself. "I didn't get their names."

Patty walked over and Grant shook her hand. "Professor Dorset, at your service. These are my students, Adam Brisk and Jane Warrington." He seemed nervous.

Jane could not tell if he knew her or at least of her. Or if he was attracted to her. Either way, it was not her business . . . yet.

Patty nodded to the two and they returned the gesture.

"And you must be Patty?" Grant asked.

She smiled. "Patty Swanson. I am the head of Wading Industries where we can only evaluate the waters but not alter them."

"Sounds like you know your limits." Grant smiled.

"Trust me. Limitations are respected at my company." Patty smirked.

Brief silence befell the group. It was not long enough to be awkward, but it was enough time for two more people to come from around another shack on the opposite side from where Patty had come from.

"Boss, this is getting ridiculous," a dark-skinned man said aloud.

"Blaine, we have to make sure that everything is working properly and can be fixed," Patty said over her shoulder.

"Lady, screw the equipment. We need to get out of here!" the other fellow said. He was an old, crusty, pale-skinned man with a Hawaiian shirt on over a blue long-sleeve shirt.

"It's safe for now. Let's just get back." Blaine pressed the notion of leaving the village further.

Patty pondered on it for a moment. She was rethinking her whole plan, and it only took her a few seconds to come to a conclusion. "Secure the equipment. We'll come back for it."

Blaine, Caplin, and Sasha all let out long exhales. They had been holding their breath while she came to a decision.

Grant was impressed. She not only was a quick decision maker, but she respected her company motto. Everyone has got to know their limitations. "What do you need from us?"

"We need a ride back to land," Patty said.

Grant rubbed his stubby chin, the bristly sound of his beard under his fingers was soothing. "I have a few questions."

"I'll gladly answer them on the way back."

"Also, we need to make a stop before we head back in. We have some damaged equipment ourselves that needs to be looked at."

"You've got a deal." Patty held out her hand.

Grant shook it, sealing their fate. "We just need to gather some stuff and we should be ready to shove off shortly."

"Nothing too heavy I hope, the boat can't handle too much extra weight."

"No, just some of our belongings. Nothing too heavy." Patty smiled.

When the four of them walked away, Jane turned to the professor. "Grant, what the heck?"

"What?!" He held up his hands defensively.

"We don't even know who these people are, much less what they are doing out here. They don't even seem to have a boat around," Jane said.

"I hav' to agree. Dis be a bit peculiar," Adam spoke up.

"It'll be fine. They don't want any trouble. In fact, it looks like they are more so in trouble than wanting to cause it," Grant said.

"How do ya mean, Professa?" Adam asked.

"Yeah, this doesn't seem as spelled out to me at all like it seems to be for you," Jane stated.

"It's pretty cut and dry. They need a ride, that's all," Grant said.

Jane was about to protest again but she saw that Patty and her team were coming over again. She kept quiet. This was Grant's show. If he wanted to risk something, that was on him.

Patty noticed the tension almost immediately. Jane's awkward stance made it seem she was uncomfortable with her professor's decision. Meanwhile, he was second guessing his decision, his eyes darting back and forth.

Thankfully, Patty had a solution. "I can compensate you for kindness."

Grant looked at Patty and then smiled. "That won't be necessary."

"Of course, it is!" She beamed. "We are wasting your time and fuel. The least we could do is give a gesture of our thanks."

Grant thought it over. "We will discuss it when we go over what happened here when we're back on the boat. For now, let's get you aboard."

"Okay!" Patty smiled.

There were no more arguments to be made, no deals to be given. Patty, Sasha, Blaine, and Caplin all boarded swiftly. They were obviously eager to get out of there. When the dinghy took off though, everyone went back to being on edge. Patty remained calm but the others were continuously peering into the water. Jane wanted to ask what the problem was but remained silent. She knew things would play out badly, just wasn't sure when or why.

Sasha jumped at a shadow in the water created by the ripples from the waves brushing against the hull. She was about to speak up, but Patty gave her a stern look. Jane could've sworn that, from the other end of the boat, she saw her mouth the words *remain calm*.

Below them things were anything but calm. The fish was exploring its unique environment; however, it was becoming overwhelmed. The mindless slaughter of ocean life was apparent, and the fish had a plentiful harvest of flesh and innards, however it still craved more. It was always hungry.

Swimming through the sea in a zigzag motion, every opportune moment it had, it would attack. Everything it saw was fair game and potentially not a threat. They were all insignificant to the fish. Just easy prey.

The whale was the hardest target it had experienced so far. Putting up a fight, the mammal fought to live to the bloody end. The fish was too quick for it, however, and was soon able to constrict its prey and feast on whatever came out. Afterwards, it burrowed inside and feasted on the dead whale's innards.

It had sensed the presence of familiar life forms approaching. They were also mammalian-type creatures but seemed to be smarter than the whale. When one got close, the fish had decided it was going to attack but the new prey had managed to slink away and get to the surface. It was up there that a new and intriguing discovery came about. It was a massive object of sorts that carried the prey away.

Now, it followed them. It was drawn to the thing powering through the water like a charging whale. However, this whale didn't need to go underwater. This presented a new challenge. How would it get to them if they were not in its domain? Stealth and surprise attacks would have to be implemented. It was the only way.

Patience was key in obtaining its prey in this case. They were not bound by the water and had a chance to escape. The fish had to strike at the opportune moment, or it would risk giving up its presence and, in turn, its meal.

Suddenly, there were sounds, songs from the sea. There were more whales, and they were close. The fish decided to ditch the amphibious prey for now and accept the challenge for the other mammals. As it charged through the ocean, it found them. They were already timid and would be easily provoked. It had to act fast if it were to slaughter the pod of seven.

The first whale charged but was stopped in its tracks with a slice of the fish's tail. Its side had a huge gash in it now and organs were spilling out. The water turned red as an egregious amount of blood poured from its stomach along with its contents. Two other whales performed the same maneuver but met similar fates. One had its back cut open, severing its dorsal fin while the other was nearly cut in half from the neck to the caudal fins. Another charged, attempted to dodge the tail but ended up getting its pectoral fin cut off along with part of its stomach.

As the remaining three began to swim away in defeat, the fish gave chase. Snapping its jaws around one of the whale's caudal fins, it managed to propel itself forward and wrap around the mammal. It constricted until it felt the expulsion of innards and the losing on its coil on the whale. The other two kept going around in circles. It was clear they were lost without their pod. Their futile attempts to stop this life form were anything but productive. Now it was time to turn tail and swim away.

They were not fast enough.

CHAPTER FOUR

It was more spacious than expected.

Aboard the *Oceanic Titan*, Patty got a good look around before her team did. The deck was at least eight feet wide and ten feet long. There wasn't any fishing rod holders but there was a small slot underneath in the far-right corner. It looked like some kind of drain. There were also a pair of cleats on the stern that seemed stable, given the condition. In fact, everything on the boat looked shiny as if it were brand new.

She then turned around and got a glance at the cabin below. It was wider than the deck but seemed less open. It was crowded with equipment and there was a two-foot opening that led down to some water. It was some kind of storage unit or tank.

There was also a steering wheel and console above where the upper deck was. Two seats with foam cushions sat adjacent to each other. The bow was also a cluster of ropes and barrels. The ship was like a thirty-foot timeline of things getting progressively less organized. It was easy to tell where they spent the least amount of time, and she was standing on it.

Grant was already onboard, having given her permission to follow him onto the boat. He had scurried up the ladder and planted himself on one of the cushioned seats. The sound of the engine starting made Sasha jump and almost lose her footing. Caplin helped her up and then he followed.

Blaine looked at Jane and Adam who were securing a dinghy for the *Oceanic Titan*. He approached. "Need any help?" He was strictly looking at Jane.

"No, we're good." She smiled kindly.

"We know how to tie a knot, yeah?" Adam looked over his shoulder with a smirk.

Blaine knew that Adam didn't really mean anything by it. He wasn't sure if Jane and Adam were in a relationship or if there was even anything there to begin with. Still, he left it alone for now. They had plenty of time to get to know each other on the ride back. He then climbed aboard effortlessly. Jane noticed how smooth his motions were. He was seaworthy and not too hard on the eyes either. His cleanly shaved black skin and bald head shone in the harsh sun, but it didn't seem to bother him. Meanwhile, Adam had a stubby goatee and a rugged look to him which she was not into.

Soon, they were all aboard and pulling away from the fishing village.

"What was the name of that island anyway?" Jane asked Caplin, who had been staring at it as she drove away.

"Dream Bounty," Caplin continued. "It used to be a fishing hot spot in the eighties. Practically fished it dry, they did. Fishermen could catch twice their load and be five feet from home. Now, it's nothing but a relic of the past."

"I see," Jane said.

She then saw Adam getting his phone out and making his way up to the bow. She didn't want to be intrusive but figured a little investigation wouldn't hurt. Slinking around the side quietly, she saw Adam out by the pulpit. He was about to go out on it to get better service. She wondered why he wasn't up at the console with Grant. He would have better service higher up.

When closer, she saw that he wasn't dialing buttons but texting someone. She figured she wasn't being too nosy at this point so asking wouldn't hurt. "What're you up to out here?"

He spun around, an ashamed look on his face. "I figuya I call outta work. By tha time we get back it'll be too dark anyway."

"That's not cool. They'll need you. Couldn't you see if you could go in later?"

Adam scoffed at the very suggestion. Instead, he turned back to his phone and continued trying to come up with a better excuse than arriving back too late. If he did that then, just like Jane said, they would call him in for a later shift at the McBurger anyway. He hated that the fast-food joint was open twenty-four hours, seven days a week.

His father put him there forcefully. It was his form of punishment after Adam ditched a meeting he was supposed to attend between some rich businessman and his family. He knew he was getting off easy, especially when he said he could keep his phone. His mother did beg for him to have it on him because he was going to be out in the middle of the ocean.

Adam looked down at the device. A sudden feeling of guilt overcame him. He wasn't sure if he should even call out now. He just wanted to ride the easy life but everyone and everything was making it too hard. It was for a reason. He had considered it before but never really thought much about it.

Now, his text halfway written, he turned the screen off on his phone and began back starboard. A voice boomed to him from above. "Adam, come up here."

The professor's tone was demanding, and he instantly became worried that Jane had ratted him out. "Yes, boss."

He hurried back and climbed up the ladder. Grant turned to him. "I need you to take over for a few."

A huge weight lifted off Adam's chest. "Yes, boss," he repeated.

The two men switched places and Grant made his way down the ladder. Halfway to the deck, he saw Patty in the cabin. He hopped off the last few steps and walked inside. She turned to him, a look of astonishment on her face. "Quite the setup you all have here."

"We try." Grant smiled.

"I can see that," Patty said and then held out a wad of cash. "For your services, Professor."

Grant smiled and crossed his arms over his chest. "That won't be necessary. Some information will be payment enough."

Patty nodded and then put the money back in her purse. "What do you want to know?"

"Well, for starters," Grant leaned against the wall of the cabin, "You said that you were there to check up on equipment. However, you didn't specify what kind of equipment."

"Experiments were being housed in tanks, plants in a makeshift greenhouse. It was all a considerably basic setup."

"Sounds like something needing to be taken care of by a group of people around the clock?"

"Blaine and Caplin do just fine."

Grant scratched his scruffy white beard. "You all seemed pretty anxious to get out of there."

"Really? I know Sasha doesn't like being isolated. She gets claustrophobic easy, you see. However, I figured the rest of us were pretty calm."

Grant thought back. Besides Caplin staring down the village like he was in a showdown in some Old Western movie, he didn't really see too many signs of fear. Concern, however, was there. "Even so, both your workers were pretty agitated when we first met them."

"Listen, Mr. Dorset. I understand you want to get to the bottom of this, but I suggest you don't. It's nothing too worthwhile anyway."

"Humor me," Grant said.

Patty looked down when she saw a green flashing light. "What's that?"

Grant followed her gaze. "It's a test tube."

"Why is it glowing green on top?"

"It signifies that it captured something."

"Captured something?" Patty inquired.

"It's my own design. It's like an underwater mousetrap."

"Looks pretty ingenious."

Grant blushed. He knew she was trying to divert the attention away from her, but she was too beautiful to be mean to. "Ya?"

"Yes. Can I get a closer look?" She bent over the tank.

"Sure, there is no harm," Grant said and knelt by the edge with Patty.

He picked up a specimen tube that was still glowing green. "This little guy must've been sucked up when I had to pull the vacuum out quickly. I didn't even notice him."

Patty examined the angel fish and smiled. It was small and had zebra stripes on its skin with a yellow nose and fin. It was no doubt a newborn. "Angelic."

"It's in the name." Grant chuckled.

They both smiled at each other.

"Why'd you have to pull up the vacuum quickly?"

Grant thought back to the weird specimen and the report brought back by Jane and Adam. "We found something."

"What'd you find?"

Patty realized she was being obvious, persistent in not telling him too much. However, she was interested in his invention and what 'weird specimen' he and his students had uncovered.

"Let me see if I can find it," Grant said as he reached over and flicked on the switch on the inside of the tank, underneath the observation hole.

The tank became alive with blue-green light created by the lightbulb and the whitish color of the tank. Several fish were inside swimming around. There were, in fact, two angel fish in there as well as a puffer fish and a few clown fish. There were also about half a dozen snails suctioned to the bottom. Then there was the odd fish out. It was like a serpent. It made Patty's blood run cold.

Grant didn't notice. Instead, he opted to share some of their other discoveries. "Adam and Jane also stumbled upon a dead orca with unusual markings."

At first, Patty didn't hear him. She was lost in a whirlwind of regret. It showed on her face, especially in her teary eyes. She fought it back and composed herself quickly. Then, she let what Grant said process. "Unusual markings?"

"Abrasions wrapped all around it. Like something rough-skinned constricted it."

He then noticed her reaction. "What's wrong?""Have you ever seen a fish like that one before?" Patty pointed down into the tank, directly at the odd one out.

"No, have you?"

She gulped and knew she was going to regret what she was going to say next. "It's a frill shark."

"A what?"

"It was a long thought extinct fish."

"What, like a megalodon?"

"No, those are gone for good. This species is extant, meaning it's still living despite having once thought to have died out."

"Darn, I always wanted to see a megalodon."

"That would be amazing but what we're after is much smaller."

"Wait, you're after this little guy?"

"That 'little guy' is only a foot long. Try something twenty times its length." Grant's eyes darted back and forth from Patty to the tank. He then shot up. Patty slowly followed. "Is it a threat?"

"No. They're really slow and sort of just lumber along," she continued. "They were first discovered in Japan in the late 1800s by some anglers. No one believed them until 2007 when it was caught on video in Shizuoka. I first saw the video in 2009. It was amazing. Something thought to be dead forever was swimming by on my computer monitor. I've been fascinated ever since." She stared off into space for a few seconds as if reflecting on her life's mission from beginning to end.

She then looked back at him. "They normally live in deep water but do sometimes come closer to the surface."

"So, you've all been afraid of a docile, two-hundred-year-old shark? Alright, Pat, I feel humored."

"There's nothing humorous about it. This is my life's work."

"Sounds to me like you're in the wrong field."

"And what field should I be in, Mr. Dorset?"

Grant shrugged. "A doctor, I dunno. Listen, if the shark isn't a threat yet there was damage to your equipment, what is the problem?"

"I am a major in marine biology with a minor in business. I didn't achieve everything to check fevers or prescribe medication," Patty snapped.

"You're not answering my questions like you promised," Grant sighed.

"I shouldn't have to explain myself to you. I offered you answers to our project, I gave them."

"Listen, Pat. No harm, no foul."

"That's Ms. Swanson to you, Captain."

Grant was about to continue the argument when he heard a familiar voice. "We here, boss!" Adam said, his thick accent riding the breeze.

The professor knocked his fist into the ceiling to signify that he heard Adam and then stormed out of the cabin. Patty let out a huge breath. She felt sorry for them. They had no idea. It was too bad though. The captain was cute. Too handsome to be mad at.

The shimmering waters calmed Grant's nerves. They always did. With the glistening surface keeping him mesmerized, he began to search through his own thoughts. He honestly wished they were back at Dream Bounty. He took a moment to appreciate the village. It was tired and used, and yet quaint. It had been used to its full effect and yet still clung on by each individual piling and plank of wood. The structure was sturdier in some spots than others, but the overall package was a fisherman's dream. Grant often wondered how lucky he'd be to have his own little spot to go fishing. Not even anything mechanical, but a section of open woods that led to a rushing stream. A place where he could catch trout and relax, focus on his fond memories, and look forward to what the next day brings.

This little village, despite its rough exterior, had boatloads of heart. From the netting covering the sides of the huts where hooks hung to the tropical faux palm trees that added an air of Hawaiian delight. As he followed Patty towards the center of the village, he noticed that the air was salty yet delightful, not at all like the occasional lump of seaweed odor that clogged the nose and dampened the senses with its pungent aroma. It was a nice mixture of sea life and fresh air.

Patty too seemed to appreciate the village given her constant gazing. She was determined to find her team but, nevertheless, she gave fleeting glances at the surrounding tropical arrangement. Grant noticed that she was staring over at the waterlogged planks that were submerged. The rising sea level was apparent, and this village was a victim of it. At least a quarter of the atoll was sinking. It was only in certain spots though and not delegated to one specific portion. In a way, it was like it was breaking apart.

No doubt it would be a pity, Grant figured Dream Bounty only had a few more months before disappearing entirely into the sea. He hoped he'd at least have time to come back and drop a line into the waters to do some fishing. Maybe live like the Indigenous people to the island did, he may even try spear fishing. He chuckled inwardly at the thought.

Even though he only caught fleeting glances of the structure, he found himself metaphorically salivating over it. His mind couldn't quite comprehend fully why. It was as if it were calling him, yearning for his presence.

Suddenly, there was a splash as some small fish broke the water. It snapped him out of his daze. He then began to reflect on his conversation with Patty. Things had gotten heated between them fast.

"I take it this happens often," Patty said as she came out of below deck.

"What's that?" Grant asked.

"Short temper . . ."

"I don't have a short temper, Ms. Swanson," Grant continued. "I am usually a very easy-going guy. However, the safety of my students is my top priority to me. I'm sure you and everyone at Wading Industries can respect that."

Patty sighed. She then looked over her shoulder at the ever shrinking Dream Bounty. "Ever since we went there, and parked our equipment in the shacks, I fear it has only been getting worse."

"Maybe it's time to relocate?" Grant suggested.

"Maybe. . ." Patty's tone gave away that she was still annoyed.

Grant didn't sink into himself though. Instead, he gave a warm smile. "I think we got off on the wrong foot."

"I'd say so."

"What do ya say, when we get back to the mainland, I take you out to dinner?" Grant almost choked on his own words but managed to stay strong with them.

Patty blushed. "I'd say you're very bold."

"Fortune favors the bold." Grant grinned.

She knew he was a hazard to the operation. His opinions were not in line with hers when it came to the project. There was still that glimmer of hope for him. She could see it in his handsome features, especially his brown eyes. She thought about it a little longer then returned the grin. "Where did you have in mind?"

"There's this excellent local joint where they serve crab, and other seafood found in the area. Cape Town is known for its fabulous underwater menu of seafood delight." Grant gave a show of hand movements to accentuate a fancy attitude.

Patty couldn't help but giggle. "It's a date."

CHAPTER FIVE

Too far.

Sasha knew what they were doing. Not at first though. In the beginning, the secretary only heard whispers, rumors of the stuff going on down in the lab. Gossip started of it being some weird hybrid experiment. For a moment, Sasha thought her friends meant the type of car. They corrected her that they were talking about a fusion between two species and laughed at her expense.

Suddenly, one day, the team packed up and left. No warning or details given. Not even Patty, her own boss, relayed the information. It must've been some kind of top secret government project. She began to get worried.

That was six months ago.

Then, a package came in for Patty. It was in a thin but sturdy box and had security tape all around it, making it difficult to open fast. She didn't want to do it but the whole thing had been nagging at her for the better part of half a year.

Inside was a CD in a case and some documents. She read some of it. The words *shark* and *living specimen* stuck out to her most. There were numbers on the front of the case as well as written on the CD. She didn't have time to decipher them and plopped the CD into her laptop. It was the early hours of the morning and Patty wouldn't be there for another hour. What she saw, scared her.

The shark slithered out of its containment, a small cage, and darted straight for the dolphin. The defenseless mammal wasn't going down without a fight though and it quickly dashed out of the way, leaving behind a small trail of bubbles that the fish burst through. It was right on the dolphin's tail. As the two tore through the water, a scientist above watched with morbid curiosity. Sasha recognized who it was immediately as Dr. Morgan Platt.

The man was beyond mischievous. She hadn't trusted him when she first met him, and she didn't trust him while watching on camera then either. Two puffs of scraggly reddish-brown hair stuck out of the sides of his head, and he wore big, rimmed glasses that made his eyes practically bulge out of his skull. He looked cartoonishly evil, inertially untrustworthy, and downright creepy, like something out of a kid's video game. *Rated E for Evil,* Sasha sometimes joked. Sasha was glad that he wasn't with Blaine and Caplin when her and Patty had arrived.

The only reason she was invited along in the first place was because of what she had seen on that video. The result still haunted her dreams, turning reality into nightmares.

The frill shark methodically stopped in its track and planned its next move. It saw that the dolphin was making its way around a corner, and it lashed out its tail right where it predicted the dolphin would maneuver. Thankfully for it and unfortunately for the viewer, the frill shark's tail sliced the dolphin's head clean off. Both halves sank to the bottom of the tank, ready to be feasted on at its leisure.

When Sasha slammed the laptop down, Patty was right there. The two had been more than acquaintances for a while now. They moved onto friendship and even lovers for a brief time. Patty didn't want to get her in any trouble, and she knew that. Still, the look in Patty's eyes haunted Sasha, sometimes even more than what was on that disk.

Patty had taken the laptop and case for the disk and had told her not to touch her mail unless she was to give it to her directly and walked out.

Now, here she was, in the middle of the Atlantic. She just prayed it wasn't for malicious intentions. Even if her life were on the line, Sasha realized that Wading Industries had gone too far and that she couldn't let this horror live any longer. She just wished she knew if her boss felt the same.

Strapping on the scuba gear for a second time, Adam wasn't happy to be heading back down there. Jane seemed content to get whatever needed to be done completed, however, the uneasiness showed on her face too.

Grant came up to them. "Just focus on the task at hand and your surroundings. Nothing else matters. Make sure you don't run low on air of course but keep your eye on the prize. If things get too crazy down there, don't hesitate to come back up."

His two students nodded.

Blaine came over, making his way around Grant who walked away and handed Jane and Adam their goggles and respirators. "Do you need any assistance down there?"

Jane thought about his offer and even looked over at the pair of extra scuba suits neatly folded in the storage box. She then remembered what the professor had said. He wanted her not to sightsee and she had to respect that. After what they found at the last stop, it all felt wrong. Still, a job had to be done.

"I appreciate the offer but. . ."

"Woohoo!" Adam's muffled voice could be heard as he backflipped into the ocean.

Jane turned to her annoying fellow student and glared at him. When he came back up and saw her expression, he knew he'd get the wrath of it all later. He gulped and then dove back down. Jane then returned to Blaine. "I appreciate the offer, but I think we're good." She smiled.

"I thought I'd offer. No worries though. Keep an eye out for buffoons. I hear they're really aggravating," he sneered.

She huffed. "You read my mind."

Following this she put her regulator piece into her mouth, turned, and hopped overboard.

A hand smacked down onto Blaine's shoulder, causing him to jump in his place. He turned to see Caplin snickering. "Looks like love at first sight."

"Oh, shut up, you old buffoon."

He raised his arms up in surrender. "Hey, we come in all different ages and color."

"Yeah, but the older you get, the less funny it becomes."

"Ah, you're just a grouch." Caplin laughed and then walked to the portside.

***

Fragments of metal were scattered across the ocean floor. It was the first thing the two noticed when they began their descent. Some were small little chunks, but others were as big as five-foot boulders; the difference was they were hollowed out and ripped apart.

Adam didn't know what to make of it as he went to inspect the damage. It was obvious it was their sensors and test tubes but the irreparable damage was so significant. It was a metallic wasteland. Pieces of smaller scrap rolled with the tide like a baby being rocked in a cradle. Others were bumping around all over the place, onto rocks and clumps of seaweed. The clearness of it all brought about the sight of the damage going on for sixty plus feet. They couldn't see further after that.

Jane just shook her head in annoyance and defeat. It would cost the college more to fix the mess than what they'd earn from students attending the marine biology course. It was the straw that broke the camel's back for Grant, and she was about ready to cry. There was no coming back from this and, what was worse, it wasn't even his fault.

Pushing a piece that looked like the glass tube that was used on the sensor to pulsate out to get readings, Adam noticed something very strange. It didn't look like any piece that belonged to the equipment. It was small and c shaped. It was almost three quarters of a circle though. The extra length looked like a hooking mechanism of some kind, like it would attach to something, and that part would help secure it. Now, it just dangled in the tide. However, it appeared that, if it were attached to something, it'd need to be taken off remotely. It was further proven by the light on the side of the object. It glowed red, much like the professor's test tubes. However, this was much bigger than what an underwater mouse trap could manage. Adam figured the red signified that the device was activated but the prey escaped.

It sort of reminded Adam of a collar. It was roughly two feet long. If it were able to uncoil, it'd be the length from his forearm up to his shoulder. He realized that he could make it a circle if he connected the bottom piece to the other side. At first, he didn't want to attempt it. However, curiosity got the best of him, and he began to bring the bottom piece up.

Jane appeared behind him, and his head spun back. She had that curious look in her eyes that she had back on the bow of the *Oceanic Titan,* and it immediately brought back the feeling of guilt he had for his actions. He decided not to open it and bring it to the surface.

Just as he was about to start his ascent, Jane pointed past him. There was a massive black object on the ocean floor. It seemed to have appeared out of nowhere. Adam almost collapsed backwards but realized that the animal, or whatever it was, remained stationary. It was too long to be a piece of equipment.

Then, a thought ran through Adam's head. *It can' be. There's no friggin' way, man.* As the two got closer, his suspicion became reality. It was a dead orca. They were astonished that it managed to drift this far. Jane felt a cold, like a ghost just danced over her grave.

Adam dared to go closer. The whale was indeed dead. This one, however, was much larger than the last. It was over twenty feet. Yet it had similar markings to the last one.

Suddenly, Jane gasped. Adam couldn't hear it, but he did see what she saw at the exact same moment. There were seven other whales floating above them.

***

"What the hell?" Caplin shouted as he stared out the portside.

Grant looked from the console and to where Caplin was now pointing. Six, no, seven dead killer whales had surfaced. All with similar abrasions on their skin and bite marks all over. It looked like a pack of serrated teeth tore chunks off with each munch.

He then focused his attention on the fish finder. Jane and Adam were still on screen, but they were in front of a massive object, another dead orca. "Shit!"

Practically sliding down the ladder, Grant ran past Blaine and knocked Patty over and grabbed the metal rod to bang the bell with. He slammed away with all his might.

"What is going on here?" Patty said, seething with anger as Sasha ran to her aid to help her up.

Grant didn't answer.

"Mr. Dorset, answer me! What is going on?!"

***

Something moved within the whale. Adam hadn't noticed it right away. The stirring within the mammal became apparent when the whole animal shifted slightly. He slowly turned and saw several little bulges grow and then shrink on its skin, little nudges. It was like something was inside, looking for an effortless way out.

He noticed that the whale didn't have too many markings on the side he was on. It was mostly just scars from whatever attacked it. He figured it must not weigh too much given how slow the current was. Acting faster than he could comprehend the right course of action, he placed his hands onto the dead orca and began to try and pull it towards him. He feared it might have been pregnant or already given birth and the calf was stuck inside.

This heroic act would make him famous, even for just a week. He knew it'd be on camera. The boat had some underwater ones strapped to the hull that were facing all directions. This was it, his big break. He would finally make his dad proud.

***

Giving up on the bell, for they were obviously ignoring it, Grant ran up to the console and towards the camera monitor in front of the second cushioned swivel chair. He turned on the channels one at a time until he came to the one focused on his students.

"What are they doing?" Blaine suddenly appeared by his side.

"Something stupid, very-*fucking*-stupid." Grant was breathing heavily.

Patty and Sasha could only stand there on the deck and stare at each other. Both knew what was down there and the implications if it attacked anyone. For all they knew, it had already killed Morgan Platt. These were civilians though and they had to be warned. Patty was about to make her way up to the bridge when Blaine and Grant gave a collective shout of surprise.

"What is that thing?!" Grant screamed.

***

By the time Adam had pulled the orca halfway off the sea floor, he realized it had been hollowed out completely. There was still something inside it though and he had to save it. No matter the strenuous action.

The frill shark burst from the orca in a speedy maneuver that made Jane screech, causing the regulator to fall from her mouth.

Adam was paralyzed with fear. Whatever came out of the whale was no calf. It shot out of it with amazing agility that caused him to fall back and drop the whale. It slowly sank back down and landed on the sandy bottom with a light thud. However, the noise was enough to attract another fish. It was a great white that was nearby, feeding on the whale carcasses.

Behind him, Jane darted for her classmate. Her adrenaline was through the roof as she grabbed him under his shoulders and began to heft him upward; the process was much easier in the water than out of it. They were halfway up when they heard a splash.

Jane looked up and saw both Grant and Blaine had dived in to reach them. Grant got ahold of Adam while Blaine grabbed Jane. They raced towards the surface where reaching hands grasped for them.

First onboard was Jane, followed by Adam. Grant quickly got on and turned back to get Blaine. Patty got to his side quickly and handed Blaine a weapon of sorts.

"Let's finish this," she said coldly.

Blaine stared at Patty with hateful eyes. He then grabbed the weapon and made his way back underwater.

"What are you doing? Get back here!" Grant shouted.

Patty grabbed Grant and spun him to face her. "What's your boats maximum weight capacity?"

"What?" Grant stuttered for a moment.

"The weight capacity, Mr. Dorset. How much can the *Oceanic Titan* handle?!" Patty shouted, attempting to snap him out of it.

"She's thirty-feet and eight-feet across. Not including all the equipment and us, maybe a thousand pounds but even that might be pushing it."

"Thank goodness. I'll only need about seventy-five percent of that."

"What? What're you planning on doing?" Jane asked.

"We're going to bring her aboard." Patty smiled.

"Her?" Grant began to put the pieces together.

The specimen they had in their tank was the offspring of the frill shark. He began to even wonder if the fish cared or if it was just happenstance that they kept bumping into one another.

"I'm not going to allow that freak of nature on my   boat!"

"There will be no trouble!" Patty stated. "Once she's sedated, she'll be snoozing all the way back to the mainland."

Grant thought it over one more time and then shook his head. "I don't like it."

"We're in this together, Grant. Whether you want to be or not."

"Then why don't we all just leave *her* be and get out of here together?!" Grant suggested.

"Because it's more dangerous if we leave her than if we just take her with us. Think of the effect she'll have on the ocean environment!" Patty was grasping at straws now, but she wasn't lying.

Grant could see that she was not. He had a tough time giving the okay. It was as if the words were stuck in his mouth.

"Let me spell it out for you, Captain. If that shark stays out here, then the whole ocean might as well sign a death warrant. Things will noticeably change within a week at most. Then drastic differences in the environment and sea life will cause humans to be without not only a food source but transporting goods by boat will become nonexistent in a year." "What did you do to that shark?!" Grant inquired.

"Evolution." Patty smiled.

There was a momentary silence before Grant nodded.

Patty reached out to shake Grant's hand, but he didn't return the gesture. "You can forget about our date," he said coldly.

"What about Blaine?" Jane whimpered.

"Don't worry, darlin,'" Caplin said. "He's wrestled with her plenty of times. He can handle her. It's the great white caught in the mix I'm mildly worried about."

"This has gone too far!" Sasha shouted.

"No, my dear. It hasn't gone far enough." Patty grinned from ear to ear. "This, as far as I'm concerned, is only the beginning. So, enjoy the show."

CHAPTER SIX

She was there.

Straight down, slithering along the ocean floor, was the frill shark. The thing was twenty feet long and covered in decay. She was an ancient looking fish, no doubt. Her lumpy head was a sign of genetic mistreatment. Bulky and battered and yet it still swam with elegance, like a thin flag blowing in the wind.

Blaine watched her from above, the surface still yielded a clear view straight down. However, wavelets would constantly brush against his chest, obscuring his vision. There was still enough clarity to see most of the bottom. He studied the fish for a few minutes, admiring her agility. He then realized she saw him, and he began to turn on the weapon, a tranquilizer of sorts that sprayed a liquid at whatever it was aiming at. It was like a flamethrower but for underwater combat.

When the first red light appeared, it signified that the device was working. It had to reach twelve to be at full capacity. Thankfully, it charged up quickly.

Beep beep beep beep beep.

It was halfway there when Blaine looked down and saw a dark shape rising straight for him. He quickly put the gun to his shoulder. It wasn't at full power, but it would have to do. He pressed the trigger and a yellow liquid jetted out. The fish didn't stop coming though. If anything, it was gaining speed. She looked larger than before, and he realized she must be zigging zagging or going in a circle to avoid the spray to get to him. Blaine began to sweep back and forth but she continued to rise.

"What's going on?!" Patty shouted.

"The damn thing's not slowing down!"

"Don't call her a *thing*!" Patty said, offended.

"She's coming up!" Sasha screamed.

The group could now see the fish rising below the surface. Their terror-stricken faces looked on with fear for Blaine. To Caplin, he was his best friend. To Patty, he was her greatest asset.

A massive black object emerged and sat there next to Blaine. He quickly realized what it was. The black and white spots, the hooked dorsal fin, all telltale signs. "It's just a killer whale!"

Adam realized instantly that the weight from the frill shark inside the dead orca held the mammal down. Now it rushed to the surface right next to Blaine. That could only mean one thing.

"She gotta be nearby! Get out of tha water, man!" Adam shouted to Blaine.

The shark wrangler suddenly didn't feel safe. In fact, he felt hunted. He obviously fell for a trap and was distracted. He had to get out of there as soon as humanly possible. Ditching the weapon, he'd worry about Patty's dismay over the gun later, he swam through the water in a climbing motion and back to the boat. One hand over the other, legs kicking, he pushed himself. Finally, he breached the surface. Afterwards, he looked like an Olympic swimmer, competing for the gold medal. Grant and Adam met him alongside the boat and pulled him up. He immediately fell onto his back, breathing heavily.

"You good?" Grant asked while giving him the thumbs up.

Blaine returned to gesture and nodded, smiling. He then looked over to Jane and grinned. Even though he had only been down there for less than five minutes, he felt like it had been an eternity since he had seen such a beautiful woman.

Just then, the boat lurched to the right. Water began to pour over the port side. However, it wasn't the frill shark's doing.

The great white sharks' sensory organs detected massive amounts of blood, splashing, and heartbeats. It was overloaded with information that its senses were trying to distinguish. Electroreceptors also detected a small, insignificant object that had sunk past it. It was going to give it a bite to evaluate it but was more interested in the objects upward. With a maneuver that caused its girth to strain, the shark shot upwards and directly at a still, bleeding object. It plowed right into the killer whale carcass and began devouring what little contents remained.

Once satisfied that there was no more meat to be secured within its jaws, it turned to the smaller object that was above the metal device that caused its senses to stir a bit. A thick, yellow fog came over the great white, but it only succeeded in sending it into a panic. The shark began to throw its head side to side, as if trying to knock the substance out of its system.

The yellow liquid had dissipated quite a bit because it had been shot out of the device for a minute now. The great white felt only slightly woozy in turn.

It set its sights on the threat above. It was charging back towards a boat. The shark didn't know what that was, but it had seen plenty before. Enough to know to be curious. A long time ago it had a feeding schedule. Boats would come and chum the waters further inland. There were several great whites and other sharks that profited from this. A memory of familiarity floated in its head. It associated the boat with food.

Charging for the puny object, it found its next target. Then, suddenly, it was gone. Homing in on the boat instead, the shark rammed into the hull.

***

"Give us a break, God! Please!" Sasha screamed.

Biting onto the starboard side, wood splintered, fiberglass cracked. The shark was going into panic mode and ready to attack anything and anyone in its way. Both Grant and Blaine noticed how unusual the shark was acting or reacting to something.

Before Blaine could, Grant approached Patty. "What was in that gun?"

Patty didn't answer.

"Seems like even a small amount of that stuff made this everyday great white go into overdrive and start attacking my boat."

She just glared at him.

"Don't you give me that look. I'm in no mood," Grant warned her.

"You wouldn't hit a woman."

"No, but I would." Jane stood by her professor. "Tell us now or I'll throw you overboard   myself."
Patty had to smirk in admiration. The poor little girl wouldn't be much of a fighter, let alone throw a decent punch. In fact, she was cute in that humble sort of way. She was innocent but had an edge of curiosity about her. If this all blew over well, she'd like to get to know her better.

"Well, we're waiting?!" Jane crossed her arms.

The shark brushed against the side of the boat, causing Patty to wobble a bit in her high heels. "Let's go inside and talk this over."

"I'm fine out here." Grant turned to Jane. "Are you alright out here?"

"Perfectly," she sneered.

Grant turned back to Patty. "No more distractions."

He was right. She was the center of attention now. All eyes were on her and she tried to put on an ashamed face. However, guilt was not one of her strong suits. She was as icy cold as her blue eyes, skating from person to person trying to find a way out of this.

"Like I already told Grant here," she gestured to the professor as if he was somehow partially responsible, "I've been fascinated by the frill shark since the early days of YouTube when footage of it premiered on their way back in the late 2000s." She continued, "It was hard to believe something like it could ever exist, especially in this day and age. I spent hours looking at old Viking stories. Similar creatures attacked them although not frill sharks. Long serpentine fish that ate their catch and swallowed their kin whole. It was so unnerving."

"Spit it out," Sasha said from behind.

Patty turned and pouted her lip. Sasha didn't seem phased in the slightest.

"Your guess is as good as mine as how they found one so large. I was told it was scouring the deep trenches in Japan, but I still couldn't figure out how it had adapted to the surface with all the light."

"Is it blind?" Jane asked.

"No, that's the miraculous part," Patty exclaimed. "It adapted thanks to the miracle of modern science. She was in a tank for a few years. The room perpetually got brighter everyday but in terribly slow succession. Soon, it just adapted naturally."

"So, what wit dis?" Adam pulled out the collar from his diving bag.

"A mind-control device. It doesn't work in the traditional sense. It allows us to read her signatures through muscle memory and, with that, we follow similar patterns to make her move around. You see, technically, she's dead."

"What?!" Caplin laughed. "A zombie shark?!"

"Sort of. In that collar is an implant. You see, she was barely alive when they brought her in. Technically, she died within three hours of being in the tank. They kept feeding her nutrients which allowed her unconscious self to somehow maintain its life. Now, when the collar broke off, she had absorbed enough of the protein to stay alive yet undead. It's only a matter of time before she is permanently deceased. That is why it is imperative that we capture her and bring her back."

"So that gun I was using wasn't a tranquilizer, but a hormone enraging distributor?!" Blaine inquired.

"Yes, that's why the healthy great white, that is making another round at us, is acting this way. Its senses have been heightened and it's not sure how to process them."

"You were trying to prolong her life?" Jane stated.

"If there is a will, there is a way." Patty exhaled. She had obviously only taken a few breaths when explaining everything.

"I've heard enough," Grant said and then made his way inside the cabin and then opened a locked chest with a key from a set he had in his pocket.

Holding up a shotgun, he walked back out onto the deck. Patty noticed this and went to stop him, but Jane got in her way.

"Who do you think you are, killing Professor Platt's project?!" Patty shouted.

Grant stopped dead in his tracks and turned to her. That last name rang a bell. "Oh, so you're part of Morgan's monstrosities? What? Is Wading Industries his new hideout?"

"He's a genius!"

"Wait, I'm lost. Who's Morgan Platt?" Jane asked.

"Trust me, you don't want to know." Sasha shuddered, thinking about the video she had seen of him.

Patty was becoming increasingly disappointed with Sasha. It was time to move on from her. "You don't see what I see?"

"Obviously not," Sasha retorted.

"Then we're through."

"Through?! Bitch we only slept together once!"

In the middle of a heated stare-off, the great white rammed into the boat. There was a resounding crack. Grant took aim and was about to fire. He didn't want to kill the shark, one of Earth's oldest living creatures, but he had to do something. The thing was hyper aggressive. "How long until that shit wears off?"

"It probably only ingested small particles of the liquid. It shouldn't last for more than five minutes. It's already been about three or four," Patty explained.

Grant practically hopped up the ladder and to the console. He started the boat and began to peel off towards the village. "She won't make it to shore. We'll have to go towards Dream Bounty."

"But we'll be back to square one!" Sasha cried out.

"It's better than the alternative."

"What's that?" Caplin asked.

"Being eaten alive," Grant said coldly.

"Listen, Professor!" Patty began. "The hormone enhancer, it has side-effects. For instance, the frill shark spontaneously grew an extra foot with a sharp blade-like protrusion that sticks out of her tail. Who knows what else will occur with her body. I do believe similar side-effects will occur with the great white."

"I want to know what the end game is here, lady?" Grant demanded.

"If the serum wears off soon enough it might not affect the great white too much. However, it could spread."

"Mutated zombie shark plague?" Caplin chuckled nervously.

"Alright, I've heard enough. It's time to head to the village and figure out our next plan of action," Grant said.

He then climbed up the ladder to the console and brought the boat around. Land straight ahead, the *Oceanic Titan* pushed through the water at a slow but steady pace. Grant looked over his shoulder and then around him, fully expecting to see the great white but it was gone.

CHAPTER SEVEN

A wreck.

The *Oceanic Titan* wobbled along as Grant pushed the throttle forward. The water onboard was becoming less and less but the starboard side hull was damaged and taking on water below where there were no drains. Grant could feel the boat wasn't going to survive another powerful hit. They had to get out of there and fast.

"Grab the bilge pumps!" he ordered his students.

Adam grabbed the one they had onboard and placed them where the water was deepest, past the bilge pump and near the stern. He set it up and turned it on then got up. A fin glided by. Adam nearly fell on his rear.

Jane looked out towards where Adam seemed startled. She saw the fin and then it turned away from the boat. "It's leaving!" she cheered.

"Oh, thank God!" Grant said.

Grant reached for the radio to call it in. He had already called in the first orca carcass but that was a few miles away. They needed assistance and the quicker the better. When he tried to reach out, he only got static. "What the?"

"What's wrong?" Caplin asked as he started to come up the ladder.

"The damn thing's not working."

"Let me see." Caplin reached for the receiver.

Grant gave it to him and watched as he looked it over momentarily. He then made his way towards the radio. After a few minutes, he stopped. "Everything's working fine."

"Then why can't I reach anyone?"

"Probably a bad zone to be in. The fishing village must be really cut off from the outside world, huh?" Caplin chuckled.

"Then how'd you get a phone call out in the first place?" Grant inquired.

Caplin looked at him funny. "We didn't get a call out."

"How did she know to come then?" He gestured to Patty.

"We used a beacon."

"Where is it?!" Jane asked excitedly. "We could use it to send an SOS to your company and get the hell out of here!"

"It's in the frill shark's stomach. The damn thing ate it," Blaine told her. "It wouldn't have mattered anyway. It only sent out a few pings before being crushed in the thing's jaws. There's no reason to even try to retrieve it."

"Shit!" Jane snapped and turned to Patty. "Why didn't you send guards or trained mercenaries? Why just you and your secretary?!"

"I came on my own accord. The team was supposed to be notified but I didn't tell them." Patty continued, "This needed to be handled as discreetly as possible. I didn't need a bunch of soldier boys running around and getting themselves and others killed!"

"Man, you guys really do test your limitations," Grant scoffed.

"Understand this, Mr. Dorset," Patty continued. "Humans will come and go but the sea will always remain. That doesn't mean I want mass extinction or a slaughter. We, as humans, must embrace our limitations and not overstep our boundaries."

"Nice speech," Adam chuckled.

"It's one I've heard all too many times," Sasha said. "It's just a plea for forgiveness. However, I'm done listening to your excuses. You brought me here for no other purpose other than you think you own me."

"That's not true," Patty said.

"Ha, bullshit," Sasha chuckled.

"Enough! We need to focus on the task at hand. "This is no time for jabs," Grant shouted.

Thankfully, no one continued.

He then drove the boat in silence. He wasn't amused by the situation at all. He then told Adam to come up. Caplin and Adam quickly traded places.

"I forgot to ask, how was the equipment down there?" Grant asked.

"Tis ruined, every-a-thing was destroyed. Pieces everywhere, man."

"Shit! Now I have to explain a damaged boat and equipment to the school!" Grant pounded his fist on the dashboard.

Adam felt sympathy for the man. He was one of the few people to help him out when he needed him most. His father would've never given him a second chance. Grant was willing to give him extra credit and he was going to earn it. Still, he felt remorse for the equipment. None of it was salvageable.

He placed a hand on the professor's shoulder. "It coulda been worse, Professa. We all still alive."

The boat rocked a bit. "Yeah, I hope to keep it that way." Grant smirked, patting Adam on the hand.

Brushing against the dock with all the grace of a bull running into a fence, the *Oceanic Titan* made it to Dream Bounty. The fishing village shook while pilings cracked from the impact. It was audible and yet, nevertheless, the dock still stood.

Jane and Adam were quick to secure a pair of lines to the pilings and brought the charter boat closer. Unpleasant scraping sounds could be heard.

Grant thought he had been lucky, dodging the rocky cove. They didn't make it unscathed though. Taking severe damage in the hull was an understatement. He managed to scrape against a coral bed and run straight into a rock right before arriving at the village. As they offloaded, the boat started listing. Caplin and Blaine stayed behind, taking buckets of water from the deck, and pouring them into the ocean.

Meanwhile, Grant began to pace back and forth. He was flustered, utterly flabbergasted. Not only was the equipment and boat ruined, but so was his teaching career. They would no doubt never let him near a boat again or a classroom. He had to make sure he could keep Adam and Jane safe; it was the only shred of hope he had left of maintaining an, at least, credible record. Not only that, but Jane was also his prized student. Without her, he'd be lost right now.

He turned to the others. "Jane, Adam. Go to the left to look for scraps of wood while me, Sasha, and Patty go right. Sheet metal works too. We need to repair the *Oceanic Titan* while we still can."

"I'll stay behind, help Caplin and Blaine," Patty offered.

"No way, lady. You're stuck with me. I have more questions about our friend out there." He turned to Sasha. "You can stay, keep guard for them."

Sasha nodded and began towards the boat.

Adam and Jane went left as instructed while Patty went straight ahead.

"Where are you going? I said to the right!" Grant was seething.

"Relax, I just need to go get something." She didn't slow her pace.

Grant was struggling to keep up. He was going to be forty this year and he was already feeling it.

Suddenly, Patty rounded a corner and disappeared. "Okay, Ms. Swanson. I'm not playing any games. Where are you?'"

He saw a curtain in place of a door ahead. It flowed in the wind like a bird feather seesawing during its descent. The wind was blowing exactly right to make it look like a creepy sheet flowing in a haunted house's window.

When he pulled it back, he saw what he would expect to find in a haunted house. A mad doctor's laboratory. Beakers and vials littered one of the tables with a dirty white cloth stretched across it. There were several rips on it. Across from that was a modern looking setup with a speaker system, knobs and switches and a set of three old bulb computers that looked like something straight out of the late eighties. Their monitors were black with green lettering running across the screens.

"It was to keep off-grid as best as possible." Grant spun around and almost clobbered Patty.

"Whoa, easy. I wasn't going to hurt you." She held up her hands defensively.

"What is all this?" Grant demanded.

He walked to the second table adjacent to the other one and saw piles of wrinkled papers. He picked some up and began to scan through them. Before Patty could grab them out of his hand, a couple of words stuck out.

"Genetically modified?!"

Patty ripped the papers away from him and looked them over. "I didn't usually come in here. This was Platt's laboratory. No trespassing."

"Bull, you're snoopy enough to want to look through the files. In fact, I bet you made a b-line for this little hut when you first arrived."

"My first obligation was to find my team. I didn't get the chance to find him or even come in here. You have to believe me!" Patty begged.

"Why should I?!" Grant shouted.

"Because I'm your only way of getting out of here now," Patty said as she pulled out a sat phone.

Adam and Jane had found a decent amount of scrap metal and wood. They carried them back with a bit of difficulty but managed to start a pile on the dock. Sasha began handing the pieces to Caplin and Blaine.

"We're going to need a lot more metal," Caplin said as he lifted his welding hat. "I would try to focus on finding it and no more wood. I'm hoping to have her fixed before mid-day."

Both the students nodded and walked back. This time they took a right. They saw Patty and Grant head straight, so it seemed like the most logical next step. It was going on eleven o' clock and time was against them.

A little ways ahead, Jane spotted something in the shallows. "Oh shit!" she exclaimed.

"What?!" Adam shrieked.

Jane gave him a humored look. She then pointed down. "Check that out."

There was a huge sheet of metal just below the surface.

"Think it could go this shallow? The shark, I mean," Jane asked.

"I dunno. I hope not," Adam said.

He was obviously apprehensive about going into the water but knew it had to be done. Jane stepped in as she held out her hand to Adam. Together, they made it in. They trudged through the warm sea, not realizing they were still holding hands. Adam liked it but Jane ripped her hand away from his grasp. The two worked in awkward silence, looking for a safe and efficient way to pick up the sheet of metal.

"Why don' we try it like dis?" Adam reached down and grabbed one of the corners.

"We should just push it. There is no sense in throwing out our backs," Jane explained.

"Da metal is pretty t'in. I t'ink it's manageable ta be lifted by human hands," Adam said, holding his hands out of the water, smiling.

"I don't know. . ." Jane said, worriedly.

"What's there not ta know?" Adam chuckled.

She blushed. He was sure being jolly. She couldn't tell if he was flirting with her or just trying to make her feel comfortable. Either way, she appreciated it.

"Here, I show ya." He knelt down and began to lift the metal up with surprising ease.

Jane began to bend over to reach for it in the shallower end. She had a firm grip on it now and she looked up at him, nodding. "Ok, let's. . . Look out!" she cried out in horror.

Behind Adam, a pair of jaws opened and snapped at him, the needle-like teeth attempting to dig into his skin. Adam fell forward in order to doge the incoming attack. He never even looked over his shoulder. He had learned the technique when his siblings would warn him that his father was about to smack him upside the head.

The two quickly sped-swam back. They were not too far out, four yards at the most. Adam stopped and scooped Jane up, practically carrying her to the docks. Meanwhile, the frill shark began to circle.

She was perpetually swimming in a wide formation. There were no signs that she was going to strike. It appeared as if she were confused on how to proceed. The prey was getting away now and she concluded at once and darted forward. Jane pulled herself upward while Adam did the same and sat down next to her. The shark didn't slow its attack though.

Quickly coiling around one of the pilings, the shark gave one quick yank, and it came loose. Adam nearly fell in the water, but Jane grabbed him by the shoulder and pulled him back. The two quickly got up and began to make their way further into the village when, suddenly, a whole heap of straw and wood landed atop them.

Grant and Patty stopped arguing when they heard the crash. Both ran out to investigate. There were more questions that needed answering but it wasn't the time now. Instead, the two ran over towards the right side of the village where the crash came from. It wasn't long before they found the source of the noise. The top of a hut had landed on his students. They were pinned down by a long makeshift beam and covered in straw. Not to mention they were soaked.

"Professor! Help us!" Jane cried out.

Both Patty and Grant ran to their aid. They struggled to lift at first; it took all four of them to lift the debris off.

Adam and Jane went to get up and brush themselves off. Grant walked up towards them. "Are you two alright?"

They nodded.

Grant then turned to Patty. "Answers, now!"

A burst from the sea caught him by surprise as well as bristly, needle-like teeth digging into his shoulder and chest. The frill shark had Grant Dorset in its jaws. Then, there was an intense pain in his back as the fish's knife-like tail impaled through his chest. Blood began to circle on his shirt. He went to scream but he coughed up the dark crimson substance instead; his lungs were collapsed. The shark then yanked backwards, pulling herself and the professor into the ocean. A cloud of blood began to form on the surface as the others looked on, petrified.

"Grant!" Jane began to run towards the water, but Adam held her back.

It was too late, he was gone.

Patty Swanson didn't know what to say. She was both shocked and amazed. The creature had a longer range and more agility than she once thought. It cost Grant his life which was horrible, but she had learned what this shark was capable of.

Jane fell to her knees and out of Adam's grasp. She began to sob uncontrollably. Adam too felt tears well up in his eyes. The two students were without their teacher and felt like aimless cubs without their papa bear. The whole trip was going south but now they felt as if they were sent straight down to hell.

What was worse was that the three could hear occasional splashes of water followed by crunching sounds. The shallows were calm enough to allow for sound to travel a decent distance. Their professor was being gorged on and they could only just sit there and take it.

The sound of footsteps coming up from behind them made everyone turn on a dime. They expected to see Sasha or even Blaine or Caplin. However, a pudgy, middle-aged, fringed looking man stood before them.

"Who da fauq are you?!" Adam asked.

"Platt." Patty grinned from ear to ear.

CHAPTER EIGHT

It was progression in quick succession.

While trying to keep an eye out for anything out-of-the-ordinary, Sasha Cane began to rub her hands on her crossed arms. She was getting worried about what was taking so long for the others to find scrap metal this time. Before, Jane and Adam had returned in minutes with a decent amount. Unless they had a plentiful bounty this time, Sasha was worried something had happened. She tried to keep her focus on what was instructed to her by Grant, but she was finding it ever so difficult. It was a gut feeling that she had. There had to be a reason for the irritation to her senses.

Caplin came out from the cabin below with the welding mask still on his head. He turned the nozzle on the torch to the off position and then lifted his head piece. He looked at Sasha, confused. They both were wondering the same thing. The others had been gone for too long and it was now going on twelve-thirty. He had to have the parts to finish the job in order for them to leave before evening and hopefully be back before dark.

Rubbing his hands together, Blaine came out from below as well. He had that look on his face that Caplin was all too familiar with. The man had an idea and made it apparent by showing his devious grin. He then reached down and pulled open a compartment under the gunwale. There was a net tucked away in there. Slowly he began to pull it out and unravel the lengthy, braided mess.

"How'd you know that was there?" Caplin asked.

"It's where I would have kept it." Blaine winked.

"What's gotten into that head of yours, Warrington?" Caplin inquired.

"Check this, we attach the fishing net to the cleats and snag the frill shark in the ropes. If we're lucky, we can burn it with the blowtorch. That shit works underwater, right?"

Caplin held the blowtorch up. "Supposedly, I mean, it hasn't fizzled out near the water below so. I'm not sure, honestly."

"Even if it doesn't, I've got something else that'll take care of our little problem." "Oh yeah? What's that?" Caplin asked, giddy and intrigued.

Blaine ducked back down below. When he returned, he unsheathed a shotgun from its casing. "I guess Grant had a spare. Guy's really prepared, huh?"

"You want to shoot the shark?"

"That or use this?" Blaine went over and pulled out a thin machete from the compartment. It had been tucked below.

"What else does he have down there?!" Caplin chuckled. "You want to stab the shark now?"

"No, I want to electrocute it."

"What're you saying?!" Caplin couldn't help but laugh.

Blaine placed the shotgun by the doorway to the cabin and held the blade aloft. "This blade has a rubber handle. If we can attach a wire or something that can cause a current, we'll give the shark the shock of a lifetime." Blaine gave a laugh that wouldn't be too far removed from someone in a stoner comedy.

"I like it. I still think you're crazy. But I like it. It's just too bad the net isn't made of metal wiring," Caplin stated.

"Close encounters of the shark kind, bro!" Blaine and Caplin fist pumped.

Blaine then looked at Sasha. "Where are the others?" he called over.

"They should've been back by now," Sasha replied.

"Yeah, you're right," Blaine said, pondering on what could have happened.

He mostly hoped Jane was okay but would be lying if he said he wasn't worried about Adam too. The guy was scrawny and thin as a rail. He just hoped he'd protect Jane if it came down to it. "Maybe they . . ." Caplin was going to offer a flimsy suggestion when a familiar face caught his attention.

Both Blaine and Caplin looked dumbfounded. "I don't fuckin' believe it," they said in unison.

Sasha was confused for a moment but then realized they were not staring at her but, rather, behind her. She spun around to be greeted by the creepy sight that was Dr. Morgan Platt. She backed up a few steps and nearly fell off the docks.

"Hold it, lady. You don't want to fall in. Unless you want to have a fate similar to that other guy."

"What other guy?" she asked.

Patty rounded the corner followed by Jane and Adam.

"Where's Grant?" Sasha asked, worriedly.

"Tha fuckin' shar' got 'im," Adam said coldly.

"How's the progress of the boat coming along?" Morgan asked, unflinching towards the others' response to Grant's demise.

"Quick," Caplin spat.

"Well, let's keep it that way. The sooner we're out of here, the better off we'll be," Morgan ordered.

"Who pu' you in charge?" Adam asked.

It was obvious the boy was agitated and just looking for a fight. Morgan did not seem to have time for his petty games however and just walked past him and back towards the center of the village, near the hut headquarters.

Sasha turned to Blaine and Caplin and mouthed the words *I thought he was dead?*

The two shrugged. They were both surprised to see the mad scientist was still kicking around and as unmerciful as ever in the village. They thought they had heard him scream and had gone to investigate. They heard a splash and saw signs of seawater splashed around. There had been no sign of the professor, though.

The last time they saw him was when he ordered them to check the equipment and investigate the strange noises. Now that he was back, it was like seeing a ghost.

"I have a plan," Blaine called out to Morgan.

"We all have plans," he sneered but kept walking with his back to him.

***

Finding the cords to cause the electrical current was the easy part. They just borrowed some wire from the console and rerouted it to the deck. Getting the net set up was another story. Caplin and Blaine both tried to untangle it, but it proved to be like bedcovers. One side of the sheet would be tucked in, or in this case unraveled, and another would pop out. The net was too thin and was continuously getting tangled. It would be perfect for capturing the shark and keeping it trapped but a challenge for the ones setting it up to begin with.

"What should we use for bait?" Caplin asked.

Blaine looked over his shoulder and at the cabin entrance. "Let's finish this then I'll bring out the worm."

Sasha and Patty stayed on the small pier while Jane and Adam looked for more weapons. There was a tension there so thick that Patty was having a tough time finding something to say without escalating the situation and running into conflict.

"I hope you realize what you've done," Sasha stated, bitterly.

Patty did not say anything at first. There was a semblance of guilt on her face, but she did not think it was too convincing. Still, there was some truth behind it. She did not want people to die, nor did she want the experiment to fail. She was about to speak when she noticed Blaine carrying a tiny, writhing animal in his hand. She recognized it instantly. "Put it back!"

Holding up the baby frill shark, Blaine turned to his employer. "Why?"

"That's a priceless specimen."

"Yeah, well you should have thought about that before creating the damned thing."

"We did not create that *beautiful creature*! We only enhanced her mother!" Patty snapped back. He reached over and picked up a small hook. Patty could not watch the revolting act of Blaine baiting the fish. Meanwhile, Sasha looked on with grim satisfaction. It was clear to Patty where Sasha's priorities lay and who she followed in terms of Wading Industries.

The frill shark wriggled and writhed in Blaine's grasp. As the hook drew closer it appeared the fish knew what its captor was doing. It tried every maneuver it could manage to escape. Blaine's grip was too tight, and it opened its mouth wide as if it were trying to let air in. There were some muscle pops in its neck that were audible to both men. Even Caplin found it hard to watch the hideous yet justified act.

Bang.

A resounding crack filled the air as a bullet flew by Patty and Sasha and grazed Blaine's shoulder. He fell back and nearly dropped the frill shark. It looped up and began to bite down on his finger. The man began to scream for dear life.

"Don't even think about it," Morgan said, holding a pistol, the report from it still causing his arm to shake.

Blaine began to panic as blood seeped from the wound. He raised his good arm and placed it over his shoulder to try and stop the bleeding. It had a bit of an effect, but it didn't stop completely. With them being miles from shore, Blaine's fears were becoming all too plausible.

There was no escape from this island and, to add insult to literal injury, he had just been shot.

Caplin went to reach over and applied pressure, but Blaine nearly kicked him away. "Just get this fuckin' thing off my finger."

His friend looked down and saw that the infantile frill shark was nibbling on his best friend's thumb. The sight was grotesque as a slime of sorts began to coat his finger and mixed with the blood. Caplin hoped it was not poisonous or contagious as he reached forward and carefully pinched the fish behind the neck which made it open its tiny jaws. As he lifted it upward, the writhing creature was having trouble trying to get out of his grip. He then walked over to the port side and was about to drop it overboard.

"Don't! We may lose it forever!" Morgan shouted.

The Hawaiian shirt wearing, old-timer turned to the scientist and grinned, his faded teeth shining with the gleam of saliva. "Not my problem, man."

Morgan stood, ready to shoot. His seething expression gave Caplin every indication that the scientist would not hesitate. The two stood in a stare-off for the better part of a minute before Caplin held up his hands in surrender. "Alright, man." He took a step forward. "You want your precious creation's abomination offspring back?"

The scientist never took his eyes off the shark spawn. Not even as it lowered slightly and then began to gain speed as it was starting to be hefted over Caplin's shoulder. "Swim for it!"

He was about to toss the thing regardless of the repercussions when the infant frill shark's mother shot out of the water. Ten of her twenty-plus foot length slithered from the shallows and now hung over Caplin, blotting out the sun. She stared at him with dumbfounded features, but it was obvious she knew what was going on. Caplin stared at her with a moment of appreciation. The size of the animal was impressive, but the features were downright nightmarish. When he thought of sharks, he always remembered them being adorable. This thing was just freakish.

Shooting forward and opening her jaws, filled with needle-like teeth, she covered his head and bit down. Blood poured down as his skull cracked. The frill shark gave a hard twist to the right and severed the man's head from his shoulders and spine.

Turning to the sound of the crunch, Blaine saw his friend standing there, rigid, like a plank of wood. He then spasmed a bit before he fell to the deck, headless. Blaine looked up further and saw Caplin's decapitated head in the bristled teeth of the frill shark. He nearly passed out from both blood loss and shock.

"Amazing." Morgan Platt grinned from ear to ear, as did Patty.

It was a faux smile, however. Patty was more repulsed than anything. More than anything else, it was a sickening sight and sound to experience. Death did not come easy for anyone; but to be torn apart by a fish. It was a new level of pain. One she wished to never experience.

Sasha could only stare on in horror as the frill shark bit down harder on the mechanic's severed head until his eyes popped out of his skull. The shark then slipped back into the water and disappeared. With that, she let out a blood curdling scream.

All the footage she had seen of the specimen paled in comparison to what had just occurred. Caplin's head was crushed under the buckling weight of the jaws and then his eyes shot out and dangled there like a pair of dice in a rear-view mirror. She was about to faint but managed to get ahold of herself long enough to regain composure.

She was not sure how much more she could take.

The infant frill shark managed to chomp down on Caplin's finger and tear it off. It then pivoted off his hand by pressing down on his palm. Shooting forward, it propelled through the air and landed into the sea. The tiny terror swam downward as it attempted to catch up with its mother. Suddenly, a red string with a jelly-like object attached to the end began to come into view. The shark snatched it and chewed it down. The eyeball made a popping sound. It felt good in the fish's mouth, and it slid down its gullet easily as well.

It then continued downward, soon reaching the bottom of the sea floor. However, it was not content with staying at the level it was at. It wanted to go deeper. Something within it drew its attention west. Abandoning its mother was no inconvenience to its mental state. It cared little for the nurturing of a motherly figure, and it cared even less about being dependent on her. So, it swam, continuously looking for a dark place to call home.

CHAPTER NINE

Darkness in the day.

Things had gone from survivable to cautious fast. Every step one took felt like the planks would creek too loud, every word said felt carried in the wind and out to sea. It was where the frill shark was waiting. She had not surfaced for an hour now and everyone was starting to get bold.

Morgan began to casually walk around. Adam noticed it was as if he did not fear the shark whatsoever. The man was insane, not only in appearance but in decision making. He was obviously culpable for the shark and its creation and, in turn, knew more than what he was letting on. Still, he was taking risks for all of them by stomping around like he was.

Adam decided that the shark was gone for all the commotion the professor was causing. She would have come back to attack with how loudly Morgan walked. Adam then managed to retrieve Blaine from the boat and lay him down. Jane returned with the cleanest towel she could find to cover his shoulder. The pain was intense even though it was just a graze.

"We need to get him up somewhere," Jane said.

"Why?" Sasha asked curiously.

"His blood is seeping through the cracks," Jane explained. "It'll only be a matter of time before that thing comes back and makes a b-line right for him."

"Don't call it a thing," Patty snapped.

"It's alright, Ms. Swanson. They don't know any better," Morgan stated. "The shark's probably too busy with its head snack to take notice."

Blaine attempted to kick the scientist, but he could barely lift his foot up more than a few inches.

"T'ere is a hut, ova t'ere." Adam pointed to the left and squinted his eyes. "I t'ink t'ere's a cot in t'ere."

Adam picked up Blaine by the legs, and Jane the head, and the two carried him into the hut.

Sasha began to follow but Patty's hand snatched her by the wrist.

"What do you want?" Sasha spun around to face her.

"Don't forget where your loyalties lie." Patty stared at her intensely.

"Not anymore." Sasha felt Patty's grip loosen when she said that and managed to shake herself loose.

She then stormed inside the hut with the others.

"Forget about her," Morgan said. "We need to focus on recapturing our little experiment.

"I think it's time for plan B," Patty stated.

"We are not doing that yet. We still need her alive."

"That shark is going to kill us all. Either that or we die of heat exhaustion or lack of food and water. Take your pick," Patty snapped.

"We've got this. If we call in the favor, we'll never see her again."

Patty looked confused at the statement. She was not sure whom or what exactly he was referring to. "If anything happens to her."

"Are you referring to Sasha or the shark?" Morgan asked, a confused look on his face.

"You know exactly who."

Morgan chuckled and smiled. "Don't forget who your loyalties lie with too now."

***

Inside the hut, Jane sat by Blaine and dabbed a wet cloth on his head as well as applied pressure with another one on his shoulder. His once pitch-black skin was taking on a faint pale complexion.

"We still need to finish this," Blaine said.

"I know but you need to take it easy for now."

"I've known Caplin for eight years. He's been my best friend through thick and thin. Now he's gone." A single tear fell down the side of Blaine's face.

He wanted to sit back up, take control of the situation. However, in his weakened state, he could not do much more than just lay there and talk. He looked around a bit and saw Adam and Sasha standing in the corner, observing from afar. "Could you please just give me a moment."

Even though Adam groaned, he and Sasha walked outside out of respect. Jane was about to get up and leave too but Blaine gently placed a hand on her arm. "Stay, please."

She sat back down and looked at the man. He was glistening with sweat and blood stained the left side of his reddish-brown shirt, but he was handsome, nevertheless.

"I've gotta ask you somthin,'" Blaine stated.

"Oh yeah? What's that?" She gave him a wry smile.

"How do you come into this world in this day and age yet look like a wholesome woman?"

Jane laughed. "I have a temper sometimes. I wouldn't call myself wholesome."

"Yeah, but like, you shine. Your curly locks and bright smile, you could pass for a porcelain doll."

She looked at him. "Porcelain dolls don't have teeth."

The two laughed.

"You have a nice smile yourself, Mr. Foster."

"It's Blaine." He smiled back. "When we get out of here, I want to take you out to a restaurant."

"Which one?"

"Whichever one you want."

"I could really go for some Italian."

"Mmm, lasagna, meatballs. . ."

"Sausage." She winked.

Blaine could not help but laugh at that. "Did you really just say that?!"

Jane blushed. "I told ya, I ain't all that wholesome."

The two laughed. Suddenly, Blaine felt lightheaded. He began to lower himself back down onto the bed and fell into a deep sleep. Jane watched him as his eyes grew heavy. She figured rest would do him good. Even though it was only midafternoon, she too felt drained of energy. Her elbow found its way to her knee, and she placed her chin in her hand. Soon, she too drifted off into sleep.

***

"I'm going back in," Sasha stated.

Adam just stood there in brooding silence.

"Are you coming?"

Adam nodded. "In a minute. I don' t'ink everythang is how it seems."

"What are you saying?" Sasha asked.

"T'ere is more here t'an jus some dead shar'."

"I don't follow."

"T'ey said that tha shar' was found in tha deep and t'at it was already that length, ya?"

"Correct," Sasha said, crossing her arms.

"I don' buy it. T'ere is more to tha story. T'ere has ta be."

"What are you trying to say? Are you implying that Wading Industries tampered with the shark?!"

"Maybe. I've seen tha way ya look at the professa. It looks like ya seen a ghost. Someone ya didn' wanna see, ya?" Adam inquired.

Sasha thought back. "I've seen classified footage of the creature in action. It tore apart its prey so mercilessly. It did not even seem to be acting out of command but rather instinct. It was like it was born to kill. However, Platt was there in every one of those videos. He saw the implications in her."

"Where did ya ge' these-a videos?" Adam asked.

"They were to be delivered to Ms. Swanson. Curiosity got the better of me and I checked them out. They were labeled weird. There were the words *test* and *run* and then some numbers afterward."

"How many numba were t'ere?"

"I don't remember the number exactly, but it was in the double digits."

"So, they been exper-a-menting with this t'ing for at leas' ten day or, at mos' ninety-nine day?"

"I can't say for certain if the numbers meant days, but I wouldn't be surprised." Sasha began to ponder on it more.

"Fish grow fas.' If its growth was somehow accelerated, t'en a fish woul' grow significantly in a shor' amoun' of time, ya?" Adam rubbed his stubby goatee. "Imma gonna go look inta dis," Adam said and began to walk away.

"Please be careful."

Adam did not reply. There was no guarantee that any of them would get out of this alive.

While he made sure the coast was clear, he began to wonder what Blaine and Jane were talking about back in the tent. There was no doubt in his mind that they were flirting with each other. Still, it did not bother him too much. She was too prudish for his taste. He liked women with a wild side to them. He never saw that in Jane.

He began to wonder if he read her wrong when she did not storm out of the hut offended by Blaine's passes. He had fully expected the sight of a prissy Jane making her way back towards the edge of the pier to see what Patty and Morgan were up to.

There were no signs of Patty or Morgan. Before he managed to sneak around the corner though something grabbed his attention through the open window. Blaine and Jane were sharing a heartfelt moment. He was not sure if they were expressing their sadness over the losses or if they were hitting on each other. Either way, it pulled at Adam's heart in two different directions. He did not feel well at the sight, so he continued.

Most of the village had open windows and doorways but one had a curtain blowing in the soft wind. It made him think that something was being hidden in there. Luring him like a siren call, he was soon pushing the curtain out of the way. What he saw intrigued him further. The archaic computers and lab setup was haunting as well as out of place on a small fishing island.

Looking over the equipment, he saw vials of dirty brown water. At least, he thought it was dirty brown water. When he knelt over and got a better look, he could see parasitic creatures swimming around in them. They were so small and insignificant, oblivious to the outside world.

He stood up and bumped into something. A needle came down and *Let Me down Easy* came on. It was not the original version though. It was a cover by one of his favorite indie artists, Paolo Nutini. The soothing voice of a female backup vocalist kicked on followed by Paolo's own vocals.

Adam stood mesmerized by the record player. He had not even seen it there. It would have been a nice reminder of the outside world, a world he wished he were back in, but it was also too loud. The trombone kicked on and the bass played rhythmically, and it was all amplified by speakers set up all around the hut.

***

"What is that?" Patty said as she finished pulling the dark grey wetsuit over her shoulder.

"That, my dear, is her favorite song," Morgan Platt huffed. It was clear then that an idea was forming. His face contorted into a mischievous grin. "This is perfect. Let's get her to break into the lab and then you can shoot her with the liquid spray."

"What if she overdoses?" Patty asked.

"She won't. If anything, she will understand more."

"Isn't that dangerous? What are the implications if that happens?"

"No, it's not dangerous. I have control over her!" Morgan shouted.

"Yeah, sure seems it," Patty said giving a sideways glance.

"Don't forget that without me, we all die."

"Without you?! Sir, all I need is to dial in that number and all the problems will go away."

"But you wouldn't do that, would you?" Morgan sneered. "We've worked on this for too long to just throw it all away. All the loss will have been for nothing."

Patty took a moment and then looked from the tracker to Morgan. "This had better work."

"Don't worry, my dear. It'll all be over soon."

***

Blaine shot up in the bed, his eyes wide with a fearful recollection. His chest heaved up and down as sweat poured down his face. Jane too straightened out. Her hands shot towards her ears as she pressed down hard.

There were speakers, two of them, at either end of the hut. They were blaring an indie pop song that was all too familiar to Blaine.

"What's going on?!" Sasha shrieked at the sudden blaring music.

"No!" Blaine said coldly and tried to get up but wheezed in pain. "Where's Adam?"

"I don't know. I mean, he went off to look for something but I'm not sure in which direction," Sasha explained.

"We have to go find him!" Blaine exclaimed.

"What is that music for?" Jane asked.

Blaine turned to her, obviously scared. "It's her dinner bell."

CHAPTER TEN

Three days earlier.

Jacob Dalton had heard enough about the project to get the gist. His understanding of the science behind it all was limited but his intentions were clear. He wanted Platt's project terminated from the get-go, but his superiors would not hear it. Now, here he was, loading an eight-foot frill shark onboard a cargo ship. The tank weighed more than any of the other containers onboard.

His friend, Trevor Morris, approached. "What? Does this thing get special treatment over weapons?"

"Nah," Jacob chuckled. "She's just a real pisser."

"Tell me about it."

"Did you have trouble getting her onboard?"

"No, but Rickshaw wasn't any help. As soon as he saw her, he began to lose it. I've never heard someone burp so much in my life," Trevor said, scowling.

"Just think of him as an intern and it gets easier to collaborate with him."

"Great. . . Babysitting." Trevor watched as three crew members secured the shark onto the deck.

The tank was moving back and forth but it held. The fish was causing all sorts of commotion and ramming her head into the plexiglass. It was an unnatural specimen, no doubt. The way she acted out of character did not go over Jacob's superior's heads. They just did not care.

"This isn't right, man."

"Hey, tell me about it. I got stuck in a mini sub with Belching Bradley all day while you got to call out sick," Trevor scoffed.

"No, I mean this project. It doesn't sit right with me at all."

Trevor thought back to hearing what the good Doc cooked up in his laboratory prior to the current experiment. Walking sharks that did not last for more than thirty-six hours, crawfish that would host in the human body as its own shell until their host immediately died. Morgan's monstrosities were the hidden underbelly of Wading Industries, the red headed stepchild no one wanted.

"What else can he create? I mean, that'll last more than two days?" Trevor asked even though he knew there was no answer. He did not even think Morgan himself knew.

"I honestly don't think I want to know," Jacob said coldly.

The two stood there as the crewmen began to unstrap the tank from the harness. Jacob did not like the look of any of it. The device was not strong enough to support the tank, the straps were too old and would rip easily. Any number of things could happen. None of them did. He inhaled deeply and then turned to Trevor. "I'll be below in the mess hall if you need me," Jacob announced.

"Alright," Trevor laughed. He could tell how uneasy his friend was but could not miss a chance to poke fun at him.

Below, Morgan Platt sat in his chambers. At his desk there were scattered papers, an overhead lamp with overly bright bulbs, and a bunch of pens. In the center was an old laptop. It was from the late nineties. He always proclaimed it was harder to detect with older equipment.

He took a draw from his cigarette and then returned to his work. His computer was transferring a few video files to a disk that featured a failed experiment. At least, it was classified as a failure. Morgan was never one to give up on a project, whether the funding ran low or out completely.

There was a lock on his cabin door. "Who is it?"

"Rickshaw, sir," Bradley said.

"What do you want?"

"I need to speak with you."

Morgan looked up from his laptop and then groaned. "Come in."

Bradley entered the room and swiftly took a seat. "I don't want to waste much of your time, sir. There is something I would like to propose though."

Visibly insulted, Morgan did not like being offered ideas that didn't pertain to his own. "This'd better be good, Rickshaw."

"I'm thinking that it'd be better for the company and for the experiment if I were to train the shark."

Morgan chuckled. "But you work with submarines, Mr. Rickshaw."

"I only do when they're in need of a fill-in. I'm more into sea life. I have studied animal behavior since I was a kid. My dad owned an aquarium."

Bradley realized that Morgan was getting impatient by his rapid finger tapping and decided to wrap it up. "I know I can have results for you in no time."

Morgan got up and walked over to the porthole. The sun beat down on his grimy face. "My guys on shore guarantee two months."

". . . And I can have it in half that time."

His boss spun on his heels. "You sound confident, Mr. Rickshaw."

"I know my animals. Much like Ms. Swanson, I am fascinated by this particular creature and have been for a long time."

"Let's make a deal," Morgan said. "You work with the shark on the mainland while my other team operates with her out at Dream Bounty."

"Done. This is perfect! I already have our working song planned."

"Working song?" Morgan raised an eyebrow.

"Think of it as a tool for commands." Bradley smiled.

The laboratory shook with the reverberations from the speaker system. Vials and beakers fell off the table and shattered, the computers began to inch closer and closer towards the edge of the desk. It was an all-out shake-off where Adam was the prize. He felt like everything was closing in around him. The noise did not help either.

Knowing the song hurt even more. It was one he used to cope with his first ever breakup. The tune helped him through tough times and now it was putting him back into one. Adam found it to be ironic in a way. The reggae-like jam was hypnotic, and he began to kneel.

Soon, his hands were over his head, and he felt his world shrink. *This can't be happening.* He was sure the song was just teasing him. Of all the songs that could have played it had to be this one.

Just then, there was a smashing sound and Adam was nearly lifted off the ground. He looked down and saw that he could see the ocean below his feet through cracks in the floorboards. He shot upright and began to back away from the center of the room.

There was a soft moment in the song where a psychedelic wobbling noise could be heard while Paolo sang. That was all there was. It was like a hypnotic hum. Then, the song kicked back on with a clap. As if on cue, the frill shark burst through the floor.

Adam fell back onto the floor. The fish quickly lowered herself and began snapping at him. He tried to kick it away, but she just kept getting closer and closer. Then, when he thought it was all over, Patty appeared behind the shark.

She began to douse her with the yellow liquid and the shark began to get agitated. Her entire sensory system went into overdrive.

"Kill tha fuckin' t'ing!" Adam cheered her on.

"Stop calling her a thing!" she screamed.

"Fine! It tha Devil!" Adam screamed back.

At that moment, Patty thought back to Grant. He seemed dedicated to his job and students, especially the latter's safety. He died so needlessly. This creature before her would do the same to the rest of them. She would not show remorse or even regret. Her life was as soulless as her eyes. Patty was about to jam the weapon into the shark's eye, finish it with an overdose, when, with a loud creak, the floorboards gave way and the two fell into the ocean.

"No!" Morgan shouted as he entered the room.

The frill shark instinctively swam to try and get away from the threat. However, when she realized her attacker was no longer an issue, she swam back and looked at her.

Observing the human that was struggling to get back to the surface, she realized it posed no harm. The shark indeed had no mercy for her. She had recognized the intentions she had possessed and that she remembered her. She had been there when the man in the white coat imprinted on her. It did not change the fact that she was just another piece of meat.

This was her time for revenge and, for her being this way, others had to pay.

Morgan saw the whole thing. The shark circled back around, examined Patty for a short while, and then snatched her around the waist. She shook her back and forth vigorously until she was ripped in two. Both parts of her sank to the bottom while the frill shark held a bunch of her now loose intestines in her mouth.

To his amazement, Morgan was fascinated by Patty's death. It was so unmerciful and vicious. The excruciating pain she must have been in before she died was no doubt catastrophic to her mind. Even though it was quick, those needle-like teeth digging in around her waist through her dark grey wet suit would have been torturous for even a few seconds. Morgan began to feel aroused by the whole thing. He had read somewhere that men were usually attracted to shiny objects. He remembered it was called magpie syndrome.

Patty's wet suit had a shine to it as did her soaked skin and golden yellow hair. But what really drew Morgan in was the blood. It had an exquisite red tint to it. Then, as the frill shark swam off with her intestines, he noticed that they shined too.

He was turned on and was not the least bit coy about it.

Adam did not notice at first. He was too shocked by the horror that had transpired. It was not until he snapped out of it and looked up that he was in disgust. "Ya fuckin' sick, man."

There was no shame in Morgan's expression. The fish had just killed his accomplice and he was turned on by it. Adam shuddered in revulsion.

Meanwhile, Morgan just had a sinister grin. It looked like he wanted more of the same, lusting for the shine, and he lunged for Adam to get it.

As quickly as a rabbit sensed something was wrong, Adam lashed out his foot and it caught Morgan under his chin. The scientist stumbled backwards. Adam then tried to get up. His hand pressed down on the record player and the vinyl made it slip away as it turned. There was a loud scratching sound to accompany the action.

He was back on the floor and was about to try again when Morgan pulled something out of his lab coat pocket. It was a small pen with a button on the side. He clicked it and a hooked knife shot out.

Adam's whole frame shook. He was scared but not about to give up. He reached up again, this time reaching across the record player. Morgan charged the man, and, in turn, he was met with a beaker smashed against the top of his head.

Blood started to spill down the scientist's cheek. He placed his hand to it and pulled back. The sight of his own blood did not arouse him as much as Patty's, but it was invigorating enough to try and strike again.

Yet he got comparable results.

Again, Adam tried to get up. His feet were slipping around on the planks of wood that consisted of the floor. The sound of glass shattering was piercing to the ears. There seemed to be no way of escape. Morgan was charging and there was no means of escape or defense. Hopefully, the pain would be quick. He turned away and was about to close his eyes.

Then he spotted it.

The student reached forward and then held a small glass object outward. The broken end of one of the nearby test tubes that had smashed on the floor stabbed into the scientist's neck. He got him bad enough to pierce the skin and for blood to spill into the glass tube. However, he did not instinctively remove it. Instead, Morgan Platt stood up and walked out of the hut as stoic as could be. It was an almost robotic walk, like Adam caused some sort of haywire in his mechanically organic make-up.

Sitting back down against the hut wall, Adam assessed the situation while trying to collect his own thoughts. Patty was gone, Morgan was insane, the others needed to be warned. It was all he could think of doing. He quickly managed to get up and walk towards the exit. He fully expected Morgan to be there to attack him, so he prepared himself by bending over when going outside and then standing back up in a defensive position.

However, Morgan was not there. What's more, there was no blood on the ground. Adam figured the tube was holding the blood in place and it just circulated back into him. Adam now had a choice to make. Warn the others right away or go after Morgan by himself. He figured that whatever the mad scientist was up to, he was already working on it. Adam figured there was not any time to waste, and he began back to the docks where the *Oceanic Titan* was.

As the song ended, so did the frill shark's interest. She did return to retrieve the legs of the woman and managed to get ahold of them down the middle and then shook them apart like a wishbone. Swallowing one, she left the other. The first leg was enough for now.

She then began to explore, swimming around pilings and pushing against the slow current. The scent of blood quickly grabbed her attention. It had been in the water for a while and was only a small amount, but it was enough. She came about and discovered there was a trail of the substance and it stopped at one specific spot.

It appeared that whatever was injured was being kept in one of the infrastructures. She could not determine were exactly. Her curiosity held as long as her attention span did. If the latter ran out, she would lose interest. Patience was one thing she mastered as an aquatic hunter. In time the prey would have to move, and the predator would be ready.

CHAPTER ELEVEN

Things were getting worse.

Jane could feel it deep within. Something had happened to Adam. First, he disappeared, then there was an explosive sound like cracking wood, now he had not returned. She could not just sit here and do nothing though. Looking over to Sasha, who appeared equally as worried, Jane decided to switch roles.

She got up and turned to Blaine. He was passed out from the pain. There was no denying that they were attracted to each other like magnets. The kinetic spark she had for him, she felt, was equally as strong to him for her. She did not want to leave him, but she had to find her fellow classmate.

Adam had turned around as well. The way he flirted with her when they were trying to retrieve the sheet of metal was cute in a way, but she felt a friendship would be a better fit for them in terms of relationships. Adam had too many daddy issues anyway.

Sasha walked over. "I'm getting really worried about Adam."

"Stay with Blaine. I'll find him." She got up and walked past Sasha.

117

"Please don't get hurt," she said.

Jane looked over her shoulder. "I'm sure everything's fine."

"How can you know?"

"Educated guess." She smiled.

Sasha knew she was lying but knew she meant well by it and let her go.

The walk around was a peaceful one. Jane had exited the hut fully expecting the worst. But the midday sun was not too aggressive and the warmth it brought was enlightening. Nothing bad could happen on such a beautiful day.

A curtain flapped in her peripheral vision. At first, she ignored it. Though something captivated her about the fabric flowing about. She did not think anything was behind that curtain but fishing supplies, some rods, a net.

She inched closer and decided to investigate further than she was originally willing. She could not explain it; deep down, she felt something terrible happened there in the past. Whether it was a few minutes ago or a lifetime ago, there was no way to tell.

Then, she remembered the cracking boards sound from earlier. It was like something exploded and broke through them. She picked up her pace and flung the curtain back.

Sure enough, there was a massive hole in the center of the room and the floor was covered in a familiar yellow liquid. It had to have been that spray Blaine had used to combat the great white.

Splintered wood was everywhere, and the water below was a murky brown. She leaned forward to get a better look. Not too close for she knew what was out there.

A head appeared before her followed by a neck, chest, arms, and then what was left of the torso. Jane could not believe her eyes. It was Patty Swanson.

Her body was half sticking out of the water and her grey wet suit was stained in blood and some strands of entrails were dangling out like jellyfish tentacles. The rest were gone.

Jane fell back onto her rear but quickly got to her feet. She then scurried out the door.

***

There was the phone. Morgan Platt snatched it off the starboard side compartment of the *Oceanic Titan*. He held it close to his face and flipped it open. The old box phone felt like a brick in his hand. He began to dial a number.

Adam, standing on the pier, knew instantly that Morgan was not calling someone. Patty would have done that by now. They would not be in their predicament had she had an effortless way out from the get-go. Morgan was sending out a code of sorts, no doubt in Adam's mind. He hopped onboard without letting his feet slam down, trying to be as stealthy as possible. Morgan had not noticed him just yet.

He began to inch closer, the scientist oblivious. Adam aimed to keep it that way until he had no other choice.

Creak.

Morgan spun around and looked Adam dead in the face. His eyes were sullen yet excited. He could not speak with the hole in his neck but his face told the student everything. Before Adam could grab the phone, Morgan hit a button on the cellular device.

In that time, Adam adjusted his aim and grabbed the test tube that was jammed in Morgan's neck. He struggled a bit, pulling it past skin and flesh. With one last mighty tug, the object was wrenched free with a hideous squelching sound.

Now bleeding profusely, Morgan struggled to find a spot to get ahold of his balance. He made his way inside the cabin where he fell into the tank. Adam decided to let him bleed out but stayed until he was gone forever, never to do this again, to create a monster.

***

After her feast, the frill shark felt rejuvenated in a way. It was as if she was satisfied but not quite. She was still in need of sustenance, but a new feeling came over her. Her sensory organs began to detect movement above her where the blood had come from, and she wanted to investigate. Being bound by the sea prevented such an act. There had been times she tried but she always registered something was off.

Now, she was gaining confidence. She had gone from eating small, bioluminescent creatures on the dark sea floor to massive mammals. These new, amphibious beings seemed craftier but, nonetheless, unaware of her presence at times.

The what ifs of the implications of entering their domain did not cross her mind because the details were too significant for her to understand. However, the desire to explore new methods of predatory styles did entice her. It was a whole different world up there. One she had always figured she was only allowed quick access to while remaining in the water.

She soon found herself wrapped around a piling and slithering upwards. Ever-weary, ever-intrigued, ever-hungry.

***

Blaine awoke with an intense pain. He then remembered the bullet that had grazed his shoulder. He cursed under his breath and then looked around. Jane was not by his side. The thought that she had gone to assist someone had crossed his mind, but he briefly wondered if they had all left him.

Just then, Sasha entered his field of vision. She was backing away from something. Blaine struggled but managed to pick his head up a bit to try and see what she saw. His eyes shot open with fright and shock.

The frill shark was in the doorway to the hut they were in. Baffled, Blaine could not even speak.

The thing can be on dry land?!

It was beyond comprehension. The whole time he, Caplin and Morgan were here, it never tried to leave its home, the sea. She knew her limitations. Now she was just casually slithering into the room.

Sasha stood petrified. She hated snakes and now a twenty-five-foot serpentine fish was making its way to her.

Blaine could not let that happen. He could not see another person die right next to him.

"Get out of here!" Blaine whispered softly.

Sasha heard but did not comprehend what he was saying. Instead, she took another step back. The frill shark, once again, slithered over.

It was a truly fragile looking creature yet it could tear your head off, no problem. It then rose above Sasha and opened its jaws wide. It was about to encompass its head and engulf her. Blaine knew she would be dead if he didn't do something. "Get out of here, Sasha!" Blaine screamed at her.

The frill shark turned to Blaine. She snarled and then shot forward and buried her head into Blaine's chest. She began to hollow him out, breaking through ribs and collapsing his insides. The fish then found her prize and ripped his heart out.

Sasha snapped out of it and turned to see Blaine disemboweled and the frill shark feasting on his insides. She broke into a run for the exit but was stopped dead in her tracks by a sharp pain in her stomach. She looked down and saw that the frill shark's tail had slipped between her legs and was now impaled through her groin and was now sticking out of her back.

She let out a horrible scream and then immediately slipped into permanent unconsciousness.

***

Jane found Adam standing over the tank in silence. The scientist, renowned for marine biology and genetic engineering, named Morgan Platt was lying face down in the contained water. She did not know what to say at first. Only one thing came to mind. "I saw Patty."

"Dis has gone fa' enough," Adam said and then turned to Jane. "Whe'e are Sasha and Blaine?"

"They're back at the hut."

"Let's get dem and get the hell outta here, yeah?"

"How?!" Jane asked, both confused and intrigued.

"We're gonna have ta list in tha open wata. I t'ink tha doc has tha village set ta explode."

"This isn't happening!" Jane shouted.

"Oh, it happenin,'" Adam said and the two began to run back to the hut.

They practically sprinted across the dock and onto the walkway. Soon, they reached the hut and stopped dead in their tracks. Sasha was at the front door with a red spot on her jeans and white blouse. She was dead on the ground, her fair skin turning paler by the second. Jane's eyes filled with tears as she ran to the doorway.

"Blaine!"

"Whatya doin,' cra-zay woman! Get back here!" Adam began after Jane.

The frill shark shot through the doorway and snapped at Jane. Adam managed to get ahold of her before the fish could chomp around her midsection and pulled her back.

"How is she on land?" Jane screamed.

"Damn'd if I know!" Adam told her and then dragged her away. "We nee' ta get tha fuck outta here!"

The frill shark had an agility that neither of them expected. She slithered after them and was behind them every step of the way. The students ran side by side and attempted to zigzag to throw the shark off. It was not working. They soon broke off and in different directions: Jane towards the boat, Adam to the lab.

At first, the frill shark was tempted to go after Jane. Her black eyes looking back and forth, she settled on Adam because he was closer. She slithered towards the spot that she remembered least. She was created and left in a test tube for a time but there was no recollection as to what she was doing there or why. Still, the objective was set. She was going to take care of them all and live in solitude on Dream Bounty Island. Then, the sound of a puttering engine got her attention. She looked back and forth and then spotted the other human trying to escape on the boat. It was a futile attempt. The boat was beyond repair at this point. The shark could sense it.

She turned back towards Adam, the prey caught in a corner, and decided to save him for later. She then charged for the boat.

Jane was looking over the phone. There was some internal clicking sound. Whatever it was, it was not going to end well when the obvious timer stopped. She saw no other option and then climbed the ladder, ascending to the console. She turned the keys and the engine roared to life. The boat began to pull away from the dock.

The frill shark slipped into the sea and slithered across the surface. She was slowly moving as if antagonizing Jane. It was only inevitable that this would go in the shark's favor. The shark came aboard, rose above the cabin and towards the console.

There was no one there.

Jane was on the bow as she kicked one of the windows open to the cabin below. The shark slithered after her quickly, but she could not fit through the window. She retraced her movements back to the console and down the ladder. She then managed to enter through the doorway and look around. Her creator's body was floating on the surface and there was an abundance of equipment. No sign of her target though.

A random bubbling sound was heard by the shark. She looked towards the tank and her creator who was obviously dead. A long metal object poked around the corpse and hit the shark in the face.

Jane tried to get out of the tank quickly but, instead, she hit the underwater lights off. Grant had forgotten to do so. Now she was plunged into darkness with the fish and Morgan.

The frill shark threw her head back and forth as blood erupted from her nostrils. She then regained her purpose and composure; the target was still here and needed to be taken care of. She looked back and she saw her creator still there, but the other human was missing. She then ducked her head in, but it was hard to see. Some of the bullet spray from Grant's shotgun had caught her in the eye. Through blurred vision she saw fish darting around and some vegetation. Then, she felt her midsection being pressed down on.

Above, Jane had hit the switch to seal off the tank. The shark was wriggling around but she could not get free. The *Oceanic Titan* shook around as Jane was flung all over the place. She managed to grab hold of a guardrail near the exit and then pulled the phone out of her shorts. She looked down at the trapped fish. "You're extinct!"

She tossed the phone at the shark and then ran outside. She hopped over the stern, right into the net Caplin and Blaine had secured. She quickly became entangled and, the more she tried to free herself, it only got worse. Her head was still above water, and she tried to reach for the cleats that held the net. She could only touch the gunwale before slipping back over the pearl-white hull.

The tank cover was starting to buckle as the frill shark fought against it with all her might. She tugged and tugged but it was a slow process. She was still making progress though.

Meanwhile, repeatedly, Jane failed to reach the cleats. Finally, she gave up and accepted her fate. She slipped under the surface and waited it out.

There was a second splash and a man plopped in next to her. She was relieved. It was Blaine. He was not dead. She thanked God and then held him. However, Blaine grabbed her and untied the net from around her body. They both then swam away just as the frill shark broke free. Free to end them. The humans' time was up. . .

And so was the bomb's.

A massive explosion rocked the *Oceanic Titan*. The fiberglass hull shattered and cracked and everything combustible inside immediately caught on fire. Sparks shot out everywhere and the frill shark was engulfed in flames. She whipped her tail around trying to latch onto anything that could pull her out of the predicament she was in. The only thing was for her to return to the sea.

Jane was laid down on the pier, what was left of it. She looked up and saw the figure standing over her. "Blaine?"

"Wha?! "Ya racis' ass mutha fuckas. We don' all look t'e same!" Adam shouted.

She chuckled and then began to cry. Adam felt her sorrow and loss and knelt next to her. She hugged him instantly and he patted her head.

There was a second explosion on the *Oceanic Titan*. It came from some of the computers and other equipment onboard. It shook the foundation of the island. One of the pilings snapped and both Adam and Jane began to slide closer towards the water below. Sticking his fingers into two planks, Adam managed to secure a grip. He then grabbed Jane by the hand.

"Geh ahol' of tha dock!" Adam shouted.

Jane managed to place her fingers like Adam's and the two began to climb. Their already slow ascension was hampered slightly by how slick the dock was. Jane's feet kept missing the gaps and her feet would slip, making a squeaking sound.

The frill shark managed to home in on the noise made by the two remaining humans and she slithered in their direction. Adam immediately noticed. "It's comin' back!"

Looking over her shoulder, Jane's eyes grew wide. It was impossible. The frill shark had survived the explosion and was now coming to finish them off. She looked up and saw Adam was already at the top where the dock leveled out. He quickly swung his legs under him and lay on his stomach. His hand shot downward and reached for Jane's.

She was having trouble getting her feet secured, much less being able to climb up the dock. All she could do was close her eyes and wince at her impending death. She did not want to give up, but the shark was too close now, merely ten yards away. Jane was situated near the end of the dock; her feet were practically touching the water still.

Realizing he could not help her the way he was trying, Adam looked around for some kind of weapon. There were none. After a few seconds, a thought crossed his mind. *Make your dad proud.* Adam quickly decided the only objective now was to save Jane. He got to his feet and dove into the sea.

"No!" Jane cried.

Adam was having a challenging time seeing underwater. The salt stung his eyes. He had become too used to swimming with the suit and gear. Still, through blurred vision, he could see the frill shark nearing. He closed his eyes and hoped to see his life flash before his eyes. However, he then wished he would not, he didn't have the best childhood. So, he wished to see the future. In his mind he saw himself dressed like his father, a dark blue suit and black tie, working hard at a desk on paperwork to provide for his family. He felt at peace.

After a few seconds, which felt like five minutes, Adam began to wonder what was happening. Did the shark leave, did it go for Jane instead? He dared to open his eyes and leave his comfort state to know what was wrong. The shark was right there; she was studying him like she had done to Patty before ripping her in half. This was it; she had waited for him to see and meet his maker.

However, the shark did not move. She was floating as if suspended in the water. She then began to rise to the surface. Her metaphorical life clock was up.

Despite this, Jane still charged for the fish with a jagged piece of broken plank in hand. She brought it down on the already deceased creature. As she punctured through its head, blood erupted from the skin. Dents were made in the skull. Jane did not slow her attack though. She mentioned the wood again and jammed it into the eye-socket of the frill shark.

Probing around, digging deeper into the brain, chunks of flesh and gouts of gore erupted. Then she fell back. She had finally exhausted all her strength. She landed right in Adam's arms, and he carried her over to the dock.

As the evening came about, so too did the beating sun. It was getting hotter now, but they were cold on the inside. Jane and Adam rested their hands behind them on the dock and watched the sunset start.

Jane looked over her shoulder and back at the village. Dream Bounty was quite a quaint area. There were around seven or eight huts in total and even some decorative palm trees that had been planted long ago. Some bridges were also around to connect the homes together. They were a way for fishermen to greet each other every morning and share catches by night.

Part of Jane did not want to leave the floating village. She wished she had been able to take notice and appreciate the minute details of the location before. With the faux palm trees and netted sidings of the shacks, it was a fisherman's utopia. She could imagine the stay-at-home wives preparing for the return of their husbands and their daily catches by getting seasonings and drinks ready. There was almost a soft singing that the wives would hum, Jane imagined.

Her aunt was a fan of pop rock and remembered a song she used to sing to her as a child. It was called *Message in a Bottle* by The Police.

Adam turned to her as she carried the chorus of the tune. She had a nice voice. It reminded him of his nanny's when she used to sing to him as a young boy. He felt warm inside. He did not necessarily want to kiss Jane. There was an overwhelming sense of respect he felt for her, though. After all they had been through, all they survived, they grew closer together as people.

She turned and smiled at him.

Sometimes, friends are better, he thought as he smiled back at her.

Suddenly, a whirring sound could be heard. They both looked to their right and saw a helicopter with the words Wading Industries on the side. Then, they turned to each other and laughed.

"Looks like they got my S.O.S." she chuckled.

"T'en t'ey mus' have some amazin' hearin'." He laughed with her.

The two stared up at the incoming chopper. Adam chuckled again. "Ya know sumthin'?"

"What's that?" Jane asked.

"I t'nk, if we make it back in time, I'll be able ta make it ta work." He gave her a smile and a wink.

CHAPTER TWELVE

Night came and went.

Adam Brisk never showed up for work. His boss called his father who was furious for the constant no-call-no-shows. The employer told him if he did that one more time he would be fired. Mr. Brisk slammed the phone down and cursed his son's name.

Jane's parents acted the complete opposite. Mister and Mrs. Warrington called her friends and other family members to try and locate her. They were not successful. They called the school who said Professor Dorset should have been back hours ago. They explained that, sometimes, equipment took a long time to fix and that the signal could be haphazard on the ocean. Her parents knew she had gone out with her professor and a fellow classmate to try and fix some of the school's equipment and that she admired and respected her professor. Mrs. Warrington feared the worst. When they called the harbormaster, he told them that the boat hadn't returned yet.

After a day of no response from either her daughter or the school, they decided to take matters into their own hands.

The police soon got involved. It was turning into town news, the big scoop on the missing teacher and his students. Mr. Brisk welcomed the publicity, but his wife was furious that he was doing it in their son's name. The whole situation was a clustered mess.

It only became worse when Dream Bounty was found. The island was almost completely submerged but signs of the *Oceanic Titan* were apparent. Pieces of gear were strewn about including a flair kit and some life jackets.

Then the biggest news came. Its source was a news chopper that was surveying around the area. The cameraman was about to look out the other door for better coverage of the island when he spotted something. It was no more than five-hundred feet from Dream Bounty.

Oceanic Titan sat idling in the current underwater. How no one spotted her before was becoming a hot topic. The coastguard got involved and a recovery operation provided plenty of wreckage but no bodies.

Just where were the professor and his two students?

***

Slam.

Adam and Jane's whole upper frames shot upward. In front of them was a file that had been deliberately smashed onto the table with aggressive force. Blurry eyed, the two survivors tried to wake up. There was no clock in the room, so they were unsure of how long they had been held captive.

Both of their sights adjusted enough to see there was a man standing before them. He looked furiously back and forth at them. His chest was heaving up and down and his face was beet red. "Do you two have any idea what you've done?!" Bradley Rickshaw spat.

The two students sat silently.

"Well, since a cat seems to be biting your tongues, I'll fill you in," Bradley continued. "I was working with that animal for the better part of two months. It was a fast learner, able to decipher right from wrong, predator from prey. It was supposed to be an easy clean up. Dr. Morgan Platt went there to recover the shark. It had been put on that floating village to be observed for its once a month, two-day visit."

Bradley strode across the room. "It must've known it was easier to escape when your destination was right outside."

He was lost in his own thoughts for a moment. "Damn thing probably studied her terrain on her first visit." He suddenly focused back on the students before him. "Now it's dead because you two killed it!"

"It had the chance to leave but it chose to stay, to kill!" Jane protested.

"Her objective was simple! Survive!" Bradley slammed his fist down onto the table.

"Right! And part of surviving is to kill. However, your fish did it with clear intentions and not instinct!" Jane shouted back.

Despite it not looking like it, Bradley did think about it. The shark had killed five people. It was uncharacteristic for a shark to commit such an act. Jane could see it on his face. "This shark isn't normal."

Their captor lifted his hands off the table and glared at the two of them.

"What'a we even doin' here, man?" Adam asked.

"This is an interrogation. I need to know what happened before the authorities have any input," Bradley said.

"I'll tell you what happened!" Jane snapped. "The shark was already acting hostile and in a frenzied state. Then, when your boss, Ms. Swanson, had chemicals sprayed at it, the thing went haywire."

"What did this chemical look like?" Bradley inquired.

Jane realized she had been leaning forward when giving her testimony on the events and calmly sat back. "I don't know. It was yellow."

"She try to kill tha damned thing wit' the stuff," Adam added.

"She wouldn't do that!" Bradley shouted. "She was just as dedicated to the project as Professor Platt."

"Give it an overdose, she tried," Adam continued, instigating the man.

"Then why didn't she?!" Bradley asked, his face contorting into one of satisfaction. He figured that Adam's story already did not add up and this would put him in the metaphorical corner.

"Because tha t'ing kill her before she coul' finish it off." Adam smiled back.

Just then, there was a knock at the door. Bradley held his stare on Adam for a few seconds before going over to it. He opened it. Jacob Dalton stood there. His eyes were stern but there was a sense of regret on his face.

"What is it?" Bradley nearly shouted.

"We've got a problem," Jacob said.

"Can't it wait?"

"I'm afraid not. It's Mr. Morgan."

Adam shot up from his chair. "He still livin'?"

"He's in critical condition. Hopefully, he'll make it through the night."

"The guy's insane!" Jane explained. "He'd sacrifice anyone for his creations."

"The wrong people, yes," Bradley said as he stared back at them. "Are you the right or wrong people?"

The two sat in their seats, on edge. Bradley left them with a guard and made his way down the hall. He and Jacob walked over towards the infirmary and opened the door.

A nurse stood by his bed while a doctor injected Morgan with a sedative. He settled down immediately. The two men walked over towards the bed.

"Can you give us a moment?" Bradley looked at the nurse and then to the doctor who nodded. "That means you too, Jacob."

His friend turned heel and exited the room without any objection. He did give a glance back over his shoulder. The old man creeped him out.

When the door shut, Bradley sat next to Morgan who was looking out at the porthole view. "This needs to be cleaned up." His voice was hoarse and raspy.

"Yes, I understand, sir. The project is still tightly under wraps for now."

"Not that, I mean. What I'm talking about is the sea   herself."
"Don't give me any of that global warming crap," Bradley groaned.

"I'm not talking about that either, damnit. Will you let me talk!" Morgan spat, nearly choking on his own words.

Bradley sat silently.

Morgan settled down a bit and then continued. "There are too many species in this ocean. It should be set back to basics. Furthermore, give the extinct creatures a good comeback. Not in a lone survivor kind of way either. The endangered species list is too damn long as it is."

"So, what're you suggesting, sir?"

Morgan was quiet for a moment. "Ya, know. I love me a good B-Movie."

"B-movie, sir?"

"You know? A b-grade movie, a bad movie. The horror genre is known for them. One of my favorites is this dinosaur flick that came out at the same time as Jurassic Park. It was called, eh, Carnosaur. The posters were, a lot of the time, better than the films themselves. The picture of a hideous T-rex standing atop some rocks over the title 'CARNOSAUR'! That shit got me excited."

"What does that have to do with the project and saving the sea?"

Morgan chuckled, ignoring Bradley's question. "What was almost as fun as the posters were the movie's taglines. For instance, Jaws 2's was *just when you thought it was safe to go back in the water.* Carnosaur's fits my desire's perfectly." Bradley gave a quick huff but gave in. "What was the film's tagline?"

His employer smiled. "*Driven to extinction. Back for revenge.*"

***

The great white swam with erratic movements. Its electrical sensory organs were going haywire, and it was picking up a bunch of things it never could before. It felt like it could sense everything in the whole ocean. The entire ecosystem was in its nostrils.

Like clockwork, it parted its jaws in a slow opening and closing fashion, engulfing everything it could. The shark sensed a lot of things that it would not have been bothered with before. Plants and underwater bacteria now made it seek cleaner water.

It required a great deal of sustenance and the only place it figured it would find it was deep down.

For many days it traveled through the Pacific, strictly westward. It had all the time in the world to find an inhabitable new home where its senses could thrive. Soon, it lowered its altitude, and the darkness began. The light from the surface quickly began to fade away as it traveled to dimmer depths.

A tiny fish slithered ahead of it. It too was heading for the depths. The great white hyper-extended its jaws, ready to swallow the fish whole. It suddenly felt a sharp pain in its side. Eyes rolling over white and teeth protruding outward, the shark began to sink. As it did, the pointed nose of a smaller predator pulled out. The great white slipped off the fish as it began to sink into the trench.

The frill shark figured it was free and began to swim at a slow pace. It was not until the jaws nearly shot out of the goblin shark in an attempt to engulf it that the prey scurried away.

The trench felt like a home that it had never known. There was no guaranteed safety, but it felt like it had a better chance down there than above.

Going in the opposite direction, the blind goblin shark began to feel something different within its bodily system. It began to shake with convulsions and spasmed into fits of twitching where its whole back end jerked forward, and its tail almost touched its head. The shark had never felt such an intense pain before.

As the great white continued to sink, blood rose. It filled the nostrils of the goblin shark and flowed through its sensory system. Before the oddly shaped predator could give into the unbearable bodily attack, the irritation ceased.

All its senses came back to it. There was the smell and taste followed by an unfamiliar one. . . Sight. The shark could now see. Its whole body felt invigorated with energy, and it sped towards the surface.

Below, a few other similar sharks fed on the great white and were soon following in the direction of the goblin shark. They too could now see and adapt to the rapidly changing water temperature.

The water was least of all clean, but it was warm, a sensation they only felt when they were too close to thermal nuclear vents.

The four sharks swam together in a shoal. They were in top form and perfect in every natural way possible.

They were alive.

🐦 @severedpress
f /severedpress

Check out other great
Sea Monster Novels!

Michael Cole
CREATURE OF LAKE SHADOW

It was supposed to be a simple bank robbery. Quick. Clean. Efficient. It was none of those. With police searching for them across the state, a band of criminals hide out in a desolate cabin on the frozen shore of Lake Shadow. Isolated, shrouded in thick forest, and haunted by a mysterious history, they thought it was the perfect place to hide. Tensions mount as they hear strange noises outside. Slain animals are found in the snow. Before long, they realize something is watching them. Something hungry, violent, and not of this world. In their attempt to escape, they found the Creature of Lake Shadow.

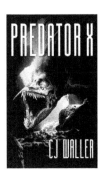

C.J. Waller
PREDATOR X

When deep level oil fracking uncovers a vast subterranean sea, a crack team of cavers and scientists are sent down to investigate. Upon their arrival, they disappear without a trace. A second team, including sedimentologist Dr Megan Stoker, are ordered to seek out Alpha Team and report back their findings. But Alpha team are nowhere to be found – instead, they are faced with something unexpected in the depths. Something ancient. Something huge. Something dangerous. Predator X

Check out other great
Sea Monster Novels!

Matt James
SUB-ZERO

The only thing colder than the Antarctic air is the icy chill of death... Off the coast of McMurdo Station, in the frigid waters of the Southern Ocean, a new species of Antarctic octopus is unintentionally discovered. Specialists aboard a state-of-the-art DARPA research vessel aim to apply the animal's "sub-zero venom" to one of their projects: An experimental painkiller designed for soldiers on the front lines. All is going according to plan until the ship is caught in an intense storm. The retrofitted tanker is rocked, and the onboard laboratory is destroyed. Amid the chaos, the lead scientist is infected by a strange virus while conducting the specimen's dissection. The scientist didn't die in the accident. He changed.

Alister Hodge
THE CAVERN

When a sink hole opens up near the Australian outback town of Pintalba, it uncovers a pristine cave system. Sam joins an expedition to explore the subterranean passages as paramedic support, hoping to remain unneeded at base camp. But, when one of the cavers is injured, he must overcome paralysing claustrophobia to dive pitch-black waters and squeeze through the bowels of the earth. Soon he will find there are fates worse than being buried alive, for in the abandoned mines and caves beneath Pintalba, there are ravenous teeth in the dark. As a savage predator targets the group with hideous ferocity, Sam and his friends must fight for their lives if they are ever to see the sun again.

Check out other great

Sea Monster Novels!

Robert J. Stava

NEPTUNES RECKONING

At the easternmost end of Long Island lies a seaside town known as Montauk. Ground Zero on the Eastern seaboard for all manner of conspiracy theories involving it's hidden Cold War military base, rumors of time-travel experiments and alien visitors... For renowned Naval historian William Vanek it's the where his grandfather's ship went down on a Top Secret mission during WWII code-named "Neptune's Reckoning". Together with Marine Biologist Daniel Cheung and disgraced French underwater explorer Arnaud Navarre, he's about to discover the truth behind the urban legends: a nightmare from beyond space and time that has been reawakened by global warming and toxic dumping, a nightmare the government tried to keep submerged. Neptune's Reckoning. Terror knows no depth

Bestselling collection

DEAD BAIT

A husband hell-bent on revenge hunts a Wereshark... A Russian mail order bride with a fishy secret... Crabs with a collective consciousness... A vampire who transforms into a Candiru... Zombie piranha...Bait that will have you crawling out of your skin and more. Drawing on horror, humor with a helping of dark fantasy and a touch of deviance, these 19 contemporary stories pay homage to the monsters that lurk in the murky waters of our imaginations. If you thought it was safe to go back in the water... Think Again!

Check out other great

Sea Monster Novels!

Michael Cole

MEGALODON VS COLOSSAL SNAKE

Brought to life by the miracle of DNA cloning, a 93-foot Megalodon shark has escaped captivity. With an insatiable appetite and unmatched aggression, it travels west for the Georgia coast, leaving a path of destruction in its wake. Bullets and harpoons can't penetrate it, steel nets can't hold it, and it's only a matter of time before the whole world finds out about it. In a race to stop the beast, the organization responsible recruit a marine biologist and a herpetologist to develop a plan to catch it. To do it, they must unleash the company's other genetically modified experiment—a 150-foot snake, resurrected from the DNA of the mighty Titanoboa. The pursuit leads to inevitable combat, and the scientists are forced to witness the deadly realities of genetic tampering. As the battle escalates, it is clear nobody is safe...and that nature never intended for these beasts to return. As the destruction mounts, and the death toll climbs, the true loser of Megalodon vs. Colossal Snake is humanity.

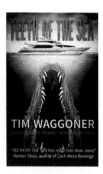

Tim Waggoner

TEETH OF THE SEA

They glide through dark waters, sleek and silent as death itself. Ancient predators with only two desires – to feed and reproduce. They've traveled to the resort island of Las Dagas to do both, and the guests make tempting meals. The humans are on land, though, out of reach. But the resort's main feature is an intricate canal system . . . . . . and it's starting to rain.

Check out other great
Sea Monster Novels!

Edward J. McFadden III
SHADOW OF THE ABYSS

Out of the past comes an immense horror. An ancient creature that must feed its voracious hunger.A massive landslide on Grand Bahama Bank sends a thirty-foot wave traveling at 150MPH toward the east coast of Florida, and the tsunami drags in something horrible from the depths of the Mid-Atlantic Ridge rift valley. Now a monster roams Florida's east coast and its shallows, searching for prey.Matthew "Splinter" Woods lives in Sailfish Haven. He's a washed-out Navy SEAL who lives off the grid on his dilapidated boat and has withdrawn from society rather than face his demons. But when his ex-girlfriend, charter boat captain Lenah Brisbee, comes to him for help, Splinter gets drawn into a battle that pits him against the strongest enemy he's ever faced as he races against time to find the monster before it turns the waters he loves blood red.

Eric S. Brown
PIRANHA

The rains came, flooding the sleepy, little town of Sylva. Sheriff Hanson never thought that he would be fighting a battle to survive against real life monsters. . .but with the waters came flesh eating, hungry creatures that swept through Sylva's streets like locusts, devouring everyone in their path.

Check out other great

Sea Monster Novels!

Michael Cole
SCAR

Scar is a killing machine. Born from DNA spliced between the extinct Megalodon and modern day Great White, he has a viciousness that transcends time. His evil is reflected in his eyes, his savagery in his two-inch serrated teeth, his ruthlessness in his trail of death. After escaping captivity, the killer shark travels to the island community Cross Point, where prey is in abundance. With an insatiable appetite, heightened senses, and skin impervious to bullets, Scar kills everything that crosses his path. His reign of terror puts him at war with the island sheriff, Nick Piatt. With the body count rising, Nick vows to protect his island community from the vicious threat. With the aid of a marine biologist, a rookie deputy, and a bad-tempered fisherman, Nick leads a crusade against Scar, as well as the ruthless scientist who created him.

Rick Chesler
HOTEL MEGALODON

An underwater luxury hotel on a gorgeous tropical island is set for an extravagant opening weekend with the world watching. The only thing standing in the way of a first-rate experience for the jet-setting VIPs is an unscrupulous businessman and sixty feet of prehistoric shark. As the underwater complex is besieged by a marauding behemoth, newly minted marine biologist Coco Keahi must face off against the ancient predator as it rises from the deep with a vengeance. Meanwhile, a human monster has decided he would be better off if Coco were one of the creature's victims.

Printed in the USA
CPSIA information can be obtained
at www.ICGtesting.com
LVHW021051181223
766765LV00035B/801

9 781922 861122